SOMEBODY ELSE'S Baby

Diane Martin

10 09 08 6 5 4 3 2 1

First Edition

Edited by Dr. William A. Martin

Printed by CreateSpace

Cover by Borel Graphics

Interior by Diane Martin

Printed in the United States

ISBN 10: 0-9802176-7-9

ISBN 13: 978-0-9802176-7-4

Disclaimer: This is a book of fiction and not based on actual events. Any similarities to current events, characters, names and locations are purely coincidental and based solely on the imagination of the author.

To all of those people mourning the loss of a loved one whose life came to a tragic end as the result of gun violence and to all of those people who stand up and fight against the injustice happening in our communities and all over the world – this book is dedicated to you.

Find out just what any people will quietly submit to and you have the exact measure of the injustice and wrong which will be imposed on them.

– Frederick Douglass

The World will not be destroyed by those that do evil; but by those who watch them without doing anything.
– Albert Einstein

Hush, little baby,

Don't say a word,

Mama's gonna buy you a mocking bird,
and if that mocking bird don't....*BANG!*

Mama's gonna buy you a
diamond...*BANG!*

And if that diamond ring don't shine,

Mama's gonna buy you a bottle
of...*BANG!*

And if that bottle of wine gets broke,

Mama's gonna buy you a Billy...*BANG!*

BANG! BANG! BANG! BANG!

Hush, little baby,

Don't say a word.

Mama's crying while her baby's dying.

Hush, little baby,

Hush, little baby,

It'll be over soon.

Hush, everyone,

Don't say a word.

Just listen…

Just watch…

Don't say a word.

Just pray and just wait.

Prologue

My name is Angel.

I am seven years old. This morning, I woke up early because it is my birthday and I am going to be a whole year older. My mommy said that she would take me to get my ears pierced if I clean up my room and guess what? I did…and I did it all by myself too. Yep, and nobody helped me. 'Cause big girls clean their own room. That's what mommy always says.

Yep, that's what big girls do and guess what else? Last night, I lost another tooth and the tooth-fairy left me two whole dollars under my pillow. I found it when I was cleaning up my room. It's a good thing I cleaned it.

I gotta tell the truth. I know there's no such thing as no tooth fairy. I saw my granny sneaking into my room and putting the two dollars under my pillow. She almost got away without me seeing her, but she hit her toe on the edge of the bed on her way out and started cussing up a storm. I looked out of the corner of my eye when I heard her say, "You son of a bitch!" Opps, don't tell her that I said that. That would really upset my granny...her being a Christian and all and I'm too little to use cuss words...even though I'm gonna be a whole year older today.

Well, back to what I was saying...oh yeah, I am so excited because I know that my mama is gonna make me a birthday cake with strawberries...so many strawberries that after eating one piece, I'm gonna turn into a strawberry. *Smiling.* I know that that is a story too, but I promise ya'…I'm gon' eat until my tummy is sooooo full. Yep, that's what I'm gonna do and my baby brother better not try to mess up my birthday…'cause I will kick his butt. He is always messing with stuff…all he does is cries and poops on himself.

I'm so excited. All I can think about is all of the gifts I am going to get. I asked my mama for a bike and she said that she was gon' get it as soon as she gets paid. Oh, I hope she got paid, 'cause I really want that bike. I dreamed about it my whole entire life. I can't wait to ring the bell on the handle-bars and I am gon' ride it all day until my hands and legs get tired.

Today, I put on my pink dress with the flowers all over it (By the way that is my favorite dress). I accidentally put on

mix-match socks. It was so funny. Boy,
everybody laughed so hard at me when
I went into the kitchen. Even my baby
brother who only goes, blah, blah, blah,
was laughing. But I don't care. 'Cause
today is my special day and nothing is
going to mess it up.

I was eating some cereal when we heard
somebody popping firecrackers outside.
I was so excited that I ran to the
window, and my mama told me to sit
down and finish my breakfast. I skipped
all the way back to my seat. My mama
saw me and said, "Sit down birthday
girl and eat your breakfast." I smiled
and did as I was told because that's

what you're supposed to do. My little brother was sitting in his big boy chair and throwing cereal all over the room. He is such a stupid-head. I don't know why God made boys. They are so yucky.

Well, I was eating my last spoonful of cereal when we heard the firecrackers again. They were making a loud popping sound. I was so happy that somebody was popping firecrackers on my special day. I was smiling and humming, "Happy birthday to me…happy birthday to me…" then I looked at my little brother, who had cereal all over his face. He smiled at me and I licked my tongue out at him. I did it when my mama wasn't looking 'cause that would make her mad and I didn't want to make her mad on my special day.

Then we heard the popping sound again. I was looking at the window when all of a sudden a hole the size of a penny showed-up out of nowhere. I was about to eat my last little bit of cereal when I looked down and noticed that my milk was turning pink – like the color of my birthday dress. I looked at the bowl and laughed a little because it looked funny to me…pink milk. I started humming my song again, when mama said, "Angel!!! No, God…not my Angel!!!"

I didn't know what mama was talking about. I started to look around the room at my mama, who was running around

like a chicken with its head cut off. I
knew that was what she was doing
'cause every time she did it…running
around like that…my grandma would
say, "Girl, will you sit down and stop
running around like a chicken with your
head cut off." My grandma was always
saying stuff like that.

"My baby! My baby!" she screamed. I
looked at my mama. She had a rag in
her hands. She ran up to me and put the
rag on my head. She looked so scared.
There were tears in her eyes. She wiped
my face, but I kept pushing her hands
away. I didn't know why she was
wiping my face. I didn't have no cereal
on it. I was careful not to get anything
on me 'cause I didn't want to get dirty.
She was crying and I didn't know why.

Then I felt something warm drop into my eye. I rubbed my face. I looked at my hand and there was red stuff all over it. I looked at my hand again and then I looked at my mommy. I didn't know what was going on.

My head started to hurt really bad. I looked up at my mama again and she really looked scared. My mama was crying and screaming. She picked me up and took me to the couch. "My baby! Lawd, not my baby!" She was crying so hard and her hands were shaking like they do when we are outside in the wintertime making 'snowmans' and snowballs. "Somebody call the police! Call the police!" she said, over- and-over again.

My grandmamma grabbed my little brother, held him close to her, while she

prayed and Lawd, was she praying. I
told them to stop crying…that it was
gonna be okay, but they told me to hush
and lay still. I did as I was told, 'cause I
didn't want to get in any trouble on my
birthday because today was my special
day.

I could hear everybody crying. They
were making such a fuss over me. Even
my baby brother. I don't know why he
was crying. Maybe, because it was my
special day and not his? Who knows
why boys do the stuff they do? I can't
really tell ya'.

I was starting to get confused about
things…like, about, where I was and
who I was. My head grew really hot and
it started to beat like somebody was
playing drums in it. Then, things got
dark like when we play hide-and-seek

and we put our hands over our eyes. I couldn't see nobody. No matter how hard I tried, I couldn't see them. My eyes were open, but 'nothing' is all I could see. It was like I was sleeping and awake at the same time. I was getting so scared and my heart was beating so fast. I reached for my mama…I reached for my grandmamma…I was trying to find them because somebody had turned out the lights. I called their names…but nobody said nothing…my mouth was moving, but I guess they didn't hear me with so much going on and all. Then my body started jumping and one-by-one, the stuff inside of me stopped working and then there was nothing.

I closed my eyes and fell asleep. I don't know why because I wasn't tired at all, but I slept. I tried to wake-up, but I

couldn't. I didn't want to go to sleep –
not today. Today was my birthday.
Then I started to dream – started to
dream about all of the people who were
coming over to celebrate my very
special day. I could see them singing
and laughing – waiting to watch me
blow out the candles and make a wish.

Well, I'm gonna sleep now. Can you do
me a favor and tell mama not to let
nobody touch my cake or my gifts…not
even my yucky little brother? He is
always putting his hands on my things.

Boy, I can't wait to wake-up. I'm so
excited about my special day and I
promise that I will be nice to my little
brother, 'cause that's what big girls
do…*Good-night*

The
Beginning...

Chapter 1

All in together...any kind of weather...I see the teacher looking out the window...what does she say? Ding, Dong, the fire bell...

My name is TKO. At least, that's what everyone calls me. At recess today, we decided to play a "friendly" game of jump rope. I say "friendly" because what starts off friendly never ends that way; especially, when you're jumping against Niecie.

As I maneuvered through the two ropes for the fifth time, I kept thinking how perfect the day was. The sun was shining bright and the only thing on my mind was how I was going beat, Niecie, at jump rope and you must understand how big that was. You see, Niecie, was the jump rope champion and she never loses to anyone, but today it looked like that might change.

As the rope swung back and forth, sweat began to drip from my face like raindrops. Niecie watched me, carefully – staring so hard that I thought her eyes would burn a hole right through me. I was beating her and to show off a little, I did a turn and a quick crisscross with my legs. I caught a glimpse of her face out of the corner of my eye. Boy, was she mad. I knew it was over, because that was my signature move – something Niecie couldn't do if her life depended on it. I did that move like I had been practicing it as far back as when I was in my mama's womb. My mother used to always tell me that even when she carried me, I wouldn't be still – "flipping and flopping all over the place."

They kept turning and I kept jumping. Niecie was fuming. She was so mad, but I didn't care. I was about to break her record and feeling confident, I stuck my tongue out and began to tease her. *Bad move.* Somehow my tongue got caught in the rope. Then the next thing I knew, I was being attacked by the rope. After hitting me in my face, on my arms and in the back of my head, the rope wrapped itself around my legs and I ended-up in a tangled mess. I hit the ground – hard. As I fought to free myself, Niecie laughed – laughed so hard, she fell on the ground. She pointed at me and called me a loser. As I unraveled myself, I said, "I got your loser, little girl." Pointing, she said, "Little girl…oh my goodness…look who's calling somebody little?" Everyone began to laugh. A small crowd was beginning to form around us. I was so embarrassed. "You are little, little girl…," I said, standing and tossing the rope onto the ground. I had dirt and grass clippings everywhere. I walked over to where she was kneeling and continued, "I bet that you can't beat this little person's butt?" Niecie stood, wiped the tears from her eyes, and then said, "You better go and sit down somewhere before your mouth write a check that your butt can't cash." Frowning, I said, "Oh, this butt can cash a check and print you a few money orders so you can go pay some bills too." The kids in the crowd said,

"Ooooooo." "Yo' mama, "she replied. "My mama, what?" I asked. She looked around before responding. "Yo' mama is sooooo stupid…" she paused and then continued, "She is soooooo stupid that she tried to put her M&Ms in alphabetical order." The crowd said, "Ooooooooooo." *That was good.* I thought to myself. I had to think of a good comeback, so I said, "Yo' mama is soooooo ugly that when she entered an ugly contest they said, 'Sorry no professionals.'" The crowd said, "Ooooooooooo." Someone in the crowd said, "Damn, she must be ugly as hell." Niecie turned to look in the crowd's direction looking for the person who made the comment, but couldn't find them and no one dared confess because they knew that she was capable of hurting somebody – real bad. Then she said, "Yo' mama is so dumb...." The crowd leaned in to hear what was coming next. "She is so dumb...," she continued. "She thought Taco Bell was a telephone company." The crowd burst into laughter. Someone said, "Man, that is one dumb mama." I looked around the crowd. Embarrassed, I didn't say anything. I couldn't say anything because I didn't have a comeback for that one, so I stood there looking confused and stupid.

We stood face-to-face; staring at each other. The other kids began to circle around us – chanting, "Fight, fight, fight!" Someone who was standing behind me pushed me into her trying to instigate a fight. Niecie pushed back. Mindful of what she could do to a person, I didn't dare touch her. We just stood there looking into each other's faces. We were so close that I could smell the pizza that we had for lunch on her breath. Neither one of us cracked a smile. We walked closer until the tips of our noses touched each other. "Fight, fight, fight!" The other kids continued to chant. After a few minutes of staring into each other's eyes, I began to laugh. I couldn't help it and she started to laugh too. We started 'cracking-up' laughing. We loved making kids think that we were going to fight, but that could never happen. Me and Niecie were so close. We made a promise that no matter what, we would never turn against each other. Never.

Chapter 2

Since January 2012, there have been more than 250 homicides in Chicago...reported in July 2012...

Niecie was my "sister from another mother." We were what air was to lungs and what sugar was to Kool-Aid...we needed each other. How we became 'friends' is sort of an interesting story. We were about five years old when we met. Niecie was the daughter of one of the most notorious women in the neighborhood. She was a prostitute turned pimp and how she got promoted is what made her notorious. When I say that her mother was made out of the same stuff nightmares were made of,

I'm being nice. She wasn't somebody that you played with and everyone knew that, but one person had to learn this lesson the hard way.

One day, after "hoeing" for twelve hours straight, it was time to check-in to tally up. It was said that her pimp had a room over at the Lakeview Motel. That's where they all met to punch-in and punch-out. Niecie's mom (Brenda was her name) and some of the other girls were seen entering the room. They said that during some arguing, a fight broke out because one of the girls came-up short and in the land of pimps and hoes that was a no-no. You see, pimps have to get their money and hoes can't make excuses for not having it.

Pimps are worse than bill-collectors. They don't care how you get the money as long as you get it. They are not trying to hear any excuses. Nope, couldn't happen and if it did all hell would break loose and on this particular night it did.

They said that her pimp started beating one of the girls really bad. I heard that he also cut the girl's face, knocked some of her teeth out before Brenda, Niecie's mama, jumped in and went crazy on his ass and I mean crazy, because another rule, from my understanding, is that you had to be crazy to go against your pimp. It was just unheard of, but she did and legend tells us that it was brutal.

The story goes on to say that Brenda pushed the pimp down onto the floor and told the other girls to run. That must have made the pimp really mad because he jumped up and began to beat Brenda – beat her like she stole something from him. Witnesses said that you could hear her screaming from the room and no one dared help. 'Cause you see, people thought that it was best to mind their own business and not get involved. Many people felt that "people" like them were from a completely different world – lived by a set of laws where if they were broken, a different set of punishments were applied. 'Those people' weren't like the rest of us, so people turned a blind-eye to what happened in their world. I never understood that, but that's how it was.

Anyway, supposedly, Brenda 'turned the tables' on him and got away somehow. She grabbed a lamp and started beating the guy. They say that after she beat him, and he lay unconscious, she cut his balls off. Cut them off with the same knife that he used to cut the other lady's face. Then she started stabbing him over and over again. After that, she set him and the room on fire and then walked out like nothing happened.

After the incident, she had his balls bronzed and until this day, she wears them around her neck as a necklace. After that, she gained much respect from the people in her world and in ours. She never went to jail for that crime. When the police investigated the crime, no one said anything. Many people thought that she was doing the community a public service by killing him, but all she did was replace one pimp with a new one; because, now, all of his girls worked for her.

All of the little girls in the neighborhood admired her. I have to admit that even I looked up to her. She didn't take no shit from nobody. Nobody played with her and it was something about her crime that made you both fear and respect her. She could have easily kept her mouth closed as her fellow employee got beaten by her boss, but she didn't. You had to be crazy as hell or just one of the bravest people in the world to do what she did. Either way, it earned her a lot of respect.

She used to ride around in a pink Cadillac with black detailing. I never understood why she chose that color for a car, but it was interesting – to say the least.

She was an interesting looking woman. She was gaudy - always draped in the official pimp's attire – a tight polyester jumpsuit, big high-heel boots, a fur coat (no matter what time of the year it was) and a lot of jewelry. She wasn't ugly or anything. She was made from the same ingredients that supermodels were made from: thin, tall, flawless skin, and cheek bones that would make any plastic surgeon envious, but what stood out most about her were her eyes – dark and set deep into her head. When she looked at you, there was nothing, but emptiness. If she didn't talk, breathe or blinked every once and a while, you would have thought the she was already dead. There was something else about those eyes. They always looked as though they were filled with tears. Those eyes saw a lot of things – a lot of painful things. Behind the darkness of those eyes were secrets – very painful secrets.

She used to talk to me all of the time. At the time, I didn't know why she chose me to open up to. Maybe, it was because she knew that I would never share her secrets. Heck, I was so little, I didn't know what a secret was, but she trusted me and at times, she would talk to me like I was her best friend…her only friend. Now, at the time, I had no idea what anything she said meant, but as I got older, her words and their meaning would become clear and important to me; important to my survival.

She once told me, "You don't want to be like me, kid, when you grow-up. This ain't no life for nobody. I have lived a hard life." She paused, lit a cigarette, took a drag, exhaled, and then looked at me, hard, like she was trying to find the right words to say. "I wasn't born to be a prostitute. It happened, just like everything else in life. You dream of becoming a doctor or a lawyer and then something happens and you end-up on your knees for some asshole who doesn't give a shit about you. Then you end-up getting so deep in the shit that you can't find no way out." I looked at her with a blank look on my face. She continued, "TKO, life is one big fucking fairy tale. That's all it is, but in my story there is no prince and no happy ending…just a bunch of toads and I've had to kiss a lot of them to make it in this world and what you see is the result. I am a product and child of the streets. I was born in the streets and will die in 'em – no happy ending for me; just an ending, but the way to have a happy ending…? Is to do what's right. Always, do what's right."

She paused, took another drag from the cigarette and then exhaled. "There's three parts to my story…to everybody's story. There is the beginning, the in-between, and the end. That's it. Don't let nobody fool you into thinking that there is more. You born…you live…and you die…that's it. You know? The key is…to do something while you're on this planet that will leave them talking about you." She paused and laughed. "People may not know you when you come, but make sure that they remember you when you leave. You know?"

I had no idea what she was talking about. "You know?" was her "thang." She ended every sentence with it. "You know?" Of course, I didn't know. I was five years old when these conversations began and the only thing on my mind at that time was graham crackers and apple juice. Plus, I don't think she even knew what she was talking about and that's why she ended every sentence with "You know?" in hopes that somebody could help her find the answer.

Every conversation ended the same way. I don't care what day of the week and no matter what we were talking about, every conversation ended the exact same way. She would take her cigarette and snuff out the ember in the ash tray. She would have a really strange look on her face. A tear would roll down her cheek and she would say, "In the end, we all…even hoes just want to be loved and respected…just like everybody else. You know?" I didn't think about it then, but when I got older, I used to think that this was odd for someone who chose "hoe" as a career choice, but she was right. Everyone wants to be loved and respected…even hoes.

But I guess the law didn't agree with her. One day, after turning a trick, one of her girls told her that a "john" refused to pay-up and pimps had to get their money. Payment was always expected when services were rendered.

When the young lady told Brenda that the man refused to pay up, they said Brenda went crazy. She found the man, in the alley, getting served by another one of her girls. They said that Brenda walked up to the car and while the girl's face was still in the man's lap, she pulled a gun from her purse, tapped on the window of the car and when the man turned and looked at her, she shouted something about love and respect and then pulled the trigger. That was the end of her career as a pimp because right after that, she left the alley and fell right into the hands of the police.

Chapter 3

Two people were found slain on the North-side...

A s a result of Brenda's actions, Niecie became motherless and of course, after hearing what happened, my mother wouldn't allow her to be placed in a foster home. She thought that by saving Niecie, God would show her favor. Not saying that foster homes are bad, but she felt that it was our obligation to help when help was needed because that's what good Christians do and my mother was, according to her, the best Christian in the world.

My mother even tried to save Brenda before she went to jail, but that would be harder than my mother would imagine. She begged her to turn her life over to God and to become saved, but Brenda found it easier to deal with the pimps in the streets instead of the ones hiding behind the "word" of God. I used to love watching my mama wave her Bible in the air, quoting scripture like she wrote the book herself. Out of respect, Brenda would listen to her, but you could tell that my mama's words were falling on deaf's ear. Brenda would always say, "Thanks for the spiritual feeding, Mrs. Owens. " Patting her stomach, she would continue, "Boy am I full, but I really need to go." That was code for, "This woman is really getting on my nerves and I wish that she would shut the hell up."

My mama could go on for hours. She loved the Lord with every pore of her being. Before we did anything, she prayed or quoted a scripture that she felt fit the occasion. When you needed a financial blessing, she would quote Psalm 37 and when you were depressed, she would quote Romans 8 31-39 and when we did something that we didn't have any business doing, she would quote James 1:22.

Everything in our house was church-related." From the music that we listened to, to the crosses that we wore around our necks, to the picture of Jesus that hung on the wall of our living room – everything, I mean everything was about God. I think she believed that the more religious memorabilia that she purchased would guarantee her more of

God's favor, but…and I may be wrong, but I think that it takes a lot more than trinkets and pictures and the ability to spit out scripture faster than the speed of light to get in His favor, but you couldn't question her faith. To do that would definitely upset her and she wasn't the type of woman that you wanted to upset.

I remember one time, a Jehovah's Witness knocked on the door. When I went to the door to answer it, I looked through the peek-hole first to see who was out there. Before I could tell her who was at the door, she opened the door and invited them in. One of the women said, "Sister, I just wanted to leave a copy of the *Watchtower* with you and…" My mother interrupted her. I dropped my head because I knew what was coming next. "Let me see what you have there." My mother took the Watchtower from the woman's hand and then said. "Come on in here and have a seat. You want to talk about God then let's talk about Him. You ladies have your Bibles don't you?" By the time my mother got done with them, they were tripping over each other trying to get out of the house. My mother could beat a person down with the "word." It was always so funny to watch the religious beat-down.

They may have all shared the truth that day, but my mother had a way of convincing you that there are only two truths – Hers and God's. I used to laugh as I watched them leave the house, exhausted, looking over their shoulders as they hurried down the driveway, shaking their heads.

I went to church every Sunday, but didn't know the "word." I always fell asleep during Sunday school and church service wasn't any different. It was something about the music, those comfortable pews, and the threat of being hurt at the slightest bit of movement that would make a child go to sleep and stay asleep until service was over.

We went to church eight days a week. Now, I know that you're saying that there are only seven days in a week, but when you are little, your concept of time is different from everyone else's. Seven days of church easily felt like eight days to a child which was the equivalent to forever.

When I was young, we weren't allowed
to watch regular TV. We watched
preachers all day long. Didn't matter
what they were talking about. We were
forced to watch it every day like folks
watched the news. My mom and dad
loved "live" sermons so much - they
would race into the living room, the
only place there was a television, and
force the rest of us to join them.

They watched it like spectators
watching a football game. They would
get so excited – shouting, "Hallelujah
and Amen!" and it wouldn't stop there.
My mother would literally stand and
cheer like the preacher discovered or
said something that they didn't already
know. I used to hate how they made us
do the "wave." If the preacher said
something exciting, my mother would

say, "Put your hands in the air….now get ready…" This was our cue to shout, "Amen!" as we waved our arms back and forth. I hated that so much. Niecie and I would just sit, with our arms stuck in the air, shaking our heads, and waiting for the cue. At times, I would imagine being somewhere else – anywhere was better than having to sit sandwiched between Mr. & Mrs. Holy-Roller with my arms stuck in the air.

At least three days a week, their worshipping would last long into the middle of the night. You could hear my mom and dad praising the Lord when most folks were sleeping. "Oh Lawd, have mercy…thank you Jesus, thank you Jezzzzzuuuuss!!!…Yes, Lawd," my father would yell over and over again and I don't know what God my mama was praying to, but she would start talking in "tongues" and screaming, "Yes, do it like the good Lawd taught you to…I'm feeling the spirit…lay hands on me baby…lay hands on me!" I used to be so glad when my daddy would finally finish "laying hands on her," because then I could finally get some sleep.

Now that I think about it, there was a lot of "laying of the hands" going on after I was put to bed. This ritual was never mentioned in church…I wonder why?

Chapter 4

Six people were shot…two killed on the South-side…

On the day of Brenda's sentencing, we took Niecie to see her mother and to say her "good-byes'. When the judge said, "You've been sentenced to life without parole, "my mother and father dropped their heads. They both began to pray. As the bailiff took Brenda away, Niecie began to scream. "No, don't take my mama!" She tried to go after Brenda, but my mother held her tightly. Before leaving the courtroom, Brenda looked at Niecie and said, "I will always be there for you…no matter what. Then she waved and mouthed, "I love you."

Niecie was crying so hard that it frightened me. "Niecie, stop it…it'll be okay…okay? Niecie…Niecie…" But she didn't stop crying. She cried all day until she fell asleep. That night, I lay awake thinking and wondering why she was crying. *Now, we can be together forever.* I thought to myself, but Niecie wasn't happy about living with us. She wanted her mama and at the time, I couldn't understand why she would prefer her mother over mine's, but as I got older, I figured it out. It wasn't that she didn't want my mama. She wanted her mama and no matter how "bad" her mother was, she was still her mama and she loved her.

After Brenda went to jail, Niecie came to live with us. The transition wasn't an easy one, and even though she was very young, growing up in an environment of prostitution and crime made her older and wiser beyond her years. My father used to tell her that she was an old woman trapped in a child's body. Niecie was hard around the edges and wasn't quick to "warm-up" to anybody. Like her mother, she didn't play and at six years old, she had already been to hell and back.

Many people talked about the men that walked in and out of Brenda's house. There was a joke in the neighborhood that Brenda's house was like a drive-thru restaurant because you could always find something hot and quick and it was always open, just like the ladies' legs; twenty-four hours a day. I could only imagine the things Niecie saw growing up, but like her mother, she would take those secrets to the grave. In their world and in our community, there was a code of silence and breaking that code could make your life very uncomfortable if the involved parties found out. What happens "in-house" stays "in-house." Now, don't get me wrong. You could talk about other folks' business, but you never...I mean never...talk about what's going on in your own house...never.

I liked Niecie because she was everything that I couldn't be. My mama ran a tight ship. In her house, you "tolled the line." The principles of respecting your parents were reenforced on a daily basis. You only spoke when spoken to. You said "yes, mam' and yes, sir." You said "excuse me" when entering a room and you always said "thank you." You respected your elders and people of authority. You never questioned why they said or did anything. It was what it was and that's even if you didn't like it, because when you're young, no one cares what you think. It was one way – their way or the highway and as a child, the highway wasn't an option.

My mother couldn't control her like she did me. She tried to, but Niecie had her own mind and she had an answer for everything. If you asked her, "Why?" she would ask you, "Why not?" This used to drive my "do it because I told you to" mother crazy. Being disrespectful was unacceptable and punishable by God's word, my mother's tirade, and my father's belt. "Spare the rod and spoil the child," is what she would say before placing you over her knee, but Niecie wasn't having it.

I remember one day, Niecie drew all over the walls in crayon. When my mother saw the writing on the walls, I thought that her head was going to explode. Her eyes grew fiery red and she was breathing through her nose like a dragon. She was so angry, she didn't even call us by name. "Get your butts in here!!!" she ordered. It was so funny to see that my daddy had joined us in the hallway – lined up against the wall by our sides. We all stood quietly as she interrogated us. "Who did this?" she asked, scowling. We all looked at each other. My father was the first to respond, "Wasn't me." My mother gave him a look that if her eyes could shoot bullets, she would have been going to jail for murder. He looked at her and then walked quickly out of the room like a man who told a dirty joke and no one got the punch line, but him. Me and Niecie were left standing there alone to suffer through what was coming next. "If we confess our sins, he is faithful and just and will forgive us our sins and purify us from all unrighteousness" (I John 1:9). When she said that, Niecie must have rolled her eyes or something because the next few words that came out of my mother's mouth came with spit attached to them. "Little girl…do you know who you are playing with?" In my mind, I kept saying, *Don't say nothing…don't say nothing…don't say…*I

didn't even finish the last thought
before I heard the word, "You" slip
from Niecie's mouth. *Oh my
goodness...you did it now.* I thought to
myself. My mother looked at me and
then pointed toward the door. I ran so
fast that I don't remember if my feet
touched the floor. When I got to the
room, I cracked the door to see what
happened next.

They stood there face-to-face – neither
one of them blinking for what seemed
like a lifetime. They were both so
stubborn that I thought that they would
be standing there until I was old enough
to drive, but soon my mother broke the
silence. "I'm going to give you a break
lil' girl because I don't think you know
any better, but try me again and I will
beat the devil out of you." After she said

that, my mother stormed out of the hallway. Niecie walked away, smiling, as if nothing had happened. Once again, David stood up against Goliath and won. I was no David or Goliath. I was the person who heard that the battle was going to happen and decided to stay in that day.

Chapter 5

25 shot over the weekend…two dead…

I was afraid of my parents, God, the police, and any other grown person that existed, while Niecie answered to or feared no one. This went on for the next eight years. My mother laid-down the laws according to the Bible and Niecie challenged every last one of them. By the time we were twelve, Niecie had broken every rule in the house and because I learned to love her like a sister, I learned how to and mastered the art of lying just to keep her out of trouble. I know that doesn't make any sense. I was raised not to lie because it was a sin, but if Niecie couldn't save herself, I felt that I had to.

I was raised to be respectful and obedient. I understood the consequences of going against my parent's rules and God's laws, but when you love someone...sometimes, you do stupid things and yes, I loved her. She was my best friend and I knew that God placed her into my life for a reason – a reason that wouldn't be explained to me at that moment, but I knew that she was important to my existence. I couldn't quite understand or explain it, but I knew that it would all be explained to me when He felt like I was ready for the explanation. In the meantime, I had to break some of the rules to keep my mother from killing her before I found out what the reason was.

One day, my mother took us grocery shopping. My mother usually insisted that we stay where she could see us, but she ran into one of the sisters from the church, so we used this as an opportunity to get away and roam around the store. When we walked passed the candy aisle, Niecie told me to keep an eye out to make sure that no one was watching. Before I could ask her why, she had placed two candy bars in the pocket of her sweater. I couldn't believe my eyes. She knew better than that, but did it anyway. If caught, not only would she get in trouble with the store's security, but she would also get into trouble with mama and I didn't want that. I begged and pleaded with her not to do it, but she was hell-bent on doing it anyway. She knew what would happen if she got caught, but she didn't care.

As we walked through the store, I was shaking like a leaf while Niecie looked cool as a cucumber. By the time we got to the register, I was sweating so bad, it looked like someone had poured a bucket of water over my head.

We were at the register, whispering, and my mother overheard us. "What are you two whispering about?" I turned and looked at her with a terrified look on my face. I looked at Niecie with eyes that begged her to do the right thing, but she lifted the corner of her mouth and smiled instead. I shook my head in disbelief. I dropped my head and waited for the madness to begin. As we approached the door to exit, I could see the security guards coming towards us from the left. My body tensed-up as if I was bracing myself – protecting myself from the impact of the moment. When the security guard said, "Excuse me, mam…" I nearly wet my pants. Confused and embarrassed, my mother asked, "Excuse me?" My eyes remained on the floor the entire time, so I can't tell you what Niecie was doing during this moment, but I can tell you this much, all hell was about to break loose. "Mam', could you come over here for a moment?" The guard requested. "No, I cannot," my mother insisted. "If you have something to say to me, say it right here…right now." The guard responded, "Well mam', one of your kids has placed some candy bars under their sweater…" At that moment, I wished that I could have been anywhere other than where I was standing. The flames in hell would have been 10 degrees cooler than the heat that was radiating from my mother's stare. Why she immediately looked at me was beyond my comprehension. She knew that I knew better, but after about 30 seconds, her stare switch directions. I was so glad because any longer and she would have burned a hole in the top of my head. She took a deep breath before speaking, "Niecie, is there something that you want to tell me?" Without batting an eye, without trying to make up a lie, she said the words that would confirm and erase any doubts about her insanity. She took the candy bars from under her sweater and then threw them on the floor. "Yeah, I took them…now what?" At that moment, I took ten steps back and another four to the left until I found myself standing next to the security guard. The next thing that happened is one for the record books. Now, as I was preparing for the Apocalypse, my mother did the unthinkable. She smiled. That's it. She just smiled. *What the hell was that?* I mean, no screaming, no throwing things or people across the store. Nothing. She just smiled, apologized to the security guard, paid for the candy bars, asked if she could take Niecie home, and after receiving approval from the management, we left.

On the way home, my mother didn't say a word and for the first time, Niecie didn't seem quite so tough. She was finally defeated. She wanted my mother to show her behind in the store. She wanted her to lose her "religion" in front of everyone, but she stayed in control. Her lack of reaction scared the hell out of me. I thought that I was afraid of my mother before that happened, but she created a whole new level of fear in me. I kept looking out of the window for a hail storm or some type of cosmic disturbance, but there was nothing that indicated we had died and went to Heaven or that I was dreaming. It was real. My mother fooled us both and for the first time in my life, I was so afraid that I knew that tonight and every night after that, I would be sleeping with the door locked and with one eye open.

That moment changed them. They weren't the same. I was riding in a car with complete strangers. The silence in the car on the way home was deafening. I kinda wished that my mama would have just knocked the hell out of the both of us – Niecie for stealing and me for not saying anything, but she didn't do anything and her not doing anything meant that she was planning something big and being nice to us in the store was a part of that plan. Maybe, she was going to kill us and bury us in the backyard? And she would get away with it too. No one would ever suspect her because she was being so nice and knowing her, if she was convicted, she would quote so many scriptures that justified her behavior that they would probably just set her free.

When we got home, nothing changed. My mother put the groceries away, told us to go wash up, and come downstairs for dinner and she smiled while saying it. Every word was drizzled with so much "sweetness" that a chill ran up my spine. Walking up the stairs was the longest walk of my life. I kept looking over my shoulder expecting something to come flying at my head, but it didn't happen.

We did what we were told and returned immediately. At dinner, my mom and dad spoke about the events of the day. As they talked, I shoveled food into my mouth like I hadn't eaten in twenty years. I couldn't wait to get away from that table, but while I rushed, Niecie picked at the food on her plate – delaying her departure from the table. I looked over in her direction and thought to myself, *She is a fool. You better get out of here.* When I stood to leave the room, my mother looked at me and with a smile she said, "Take your shower and don't forget to say your prayers before you go to sleep." *What the hell? Was that a threat? Was she going to kill me while I was praying or were her plans to get me in my sleep?* I didn't know if it was or not, but I decided to take every precaution and sleep with BOTH eyes open.

Niecie stayed behind and didn't come to bed for another hour. When I asked her what took her so long, she said, "Mind your own business and go to sleep." I looked at her like she had lost her mind. "What? What do you mean mind you own business? What are you talking about? Why are you mad at me? I didn't rat on you…you got caught." Scowling, she said, "I got caught because your

scaredy-butt was acting all
stupid…making all of those faces and
whispering." *Oh no, she didn't.* I thought
to myself. I slid to the edge of my bed. I
was about to kick that girl's butt and I
didn't care if I got in trouble. I knew that
I protected her thieving-behind and she
wasn't gon' act like I was the reason that
she got caught. I replied, "You better
check yourself…I don't know what
you're smoking, but I didn't tell your
stupid butt to steal that stuff in the first
place…mama says…" Walking up to
me, she interrupted, "YO' Mama always
got some shit to say." I covered my
mouth and said, "Ooooooooo, you
better stop cussing or you're going to
get in trouble." Grabbing her sweater,
she said, "Forget you and your mama.
Y'all are a bunch of boot-legged
Huxtable wanna-bes…you need to

remind your mama that she's not
perfect and she lives only a few blocks
away from the SHIT that she's trying to
protect you from…shoot I'm a part of
the shit that she hates and snubs her
nose at. She had the nerve to put me on
punishment. Who the hell she thinks she
is…Warden Owens? Man, this prisoner
is about to break free of this bullshit. Let
her preach that dumbshit to you…and
when you see her again, tell her that no
one is perfect other than the God she
serves and He doesn't like ugly and
don't care too much about beauty." She
said a mouthful and by the time I was
able to collect my thoughts to make sure
that I had a good comeback, she was out
of the window and into the darkness.

Chapter 6

Three people were shot in the Grand Crossing Area...

I didn't know what to do. My mother would punish me if I didn't tell her that Niecie was gone and God forbid if something happened to her, my mother would have been so mad at me, so I went into their bedroom to tell them what happened. When I walked in, I had walked into a situation that I wasn't quite ready for. I don't know if this is what you call "laying hands on somebody," but they were doing something and it was completely different from what I thought they were doing late at night after I went to bed.

They were naked and my mother was jumping up and down on top of my father like she was riding one of those mechanical horses that sat outside of the grocery store. They were both screaming, so I ran over to help them, but when I got closer it looked like my father was really enjoying the fact that my mother was bouncing all over him, so I turned to leave the room and in the process I accidentally kicked one of my father's slippers. They both turned and with a look of horror on their faces, they jumped up and began to cover themselves.

"What are you doing? Why aren't you in bed?" My mother asked as she searched for her clothing. My father on the other hand seemed too out of breath to speak. He just laid there with his hand on his chest and his mouth hanging open. "I asked you a question. Why aren't you in bed?" my mother asked, again. Trying to shake the image from my mind, I covered my eyes, and I shouted, "Niecie ran away!" I made an opening in my fingers to see what was going on, but then became distracted again as I caught a glimpse of my parent's naked bodies. I shuddered. The image was frightening and I knew that it would one day serve as the foundation for future therapy sessions.

"What? She did what?" Now, my father started to move. "Where did she go?" He stood to grab his pants. I quickly turned around, but not fast enough because I saw his butt and it was gross. It looked like a fuzzy peach with a line running through it. That image would haunt me for the rest of my life.

After he put on his pants and my mother grabbed her purse and keys we all ran from the house toward the door. When we got to the driveway, we were stopped by the sound of someone crying in the distance. "What is that?" my mother asked. "Shhhhhh…." My father said. We followed the sound to the backyard where we found Niecie crying. We all started walking toward her, when my mother stopped us and then said, "You two go into the house and I will handle this." "Are you sure?" my father asked. "Yeah, I'm sure," she said.

My dad and I were walking toward the house, but decided to hide behind a bush to see how my mother was going to handle this. Surprisingly, my mother didn't say a word. She just sat down beside Niecie, wrapped her arms around her, and said nothing. Niecie did all of the talking.

"I left and realized that I had nowhere else to go. No one to care about me…no one to love me…no one," she said, as she wiped tears from her eyes. Finally my mother broke her silence and said, "I can't tell you that I understand what you are going through because I don't know. Only you know what you're feeling, but I can tell you that you're going about this all wrong. You're trying to find something or someone that doesn't exist anymore. You're holding on to a past that held a lot of pain for you, but that was your past. You can't use those experiences to act out against the people who are trying to love you. Maybe you miss your mother…I don't know if that's it, and I know that I didn't give birth to you, but you're my baby now. You don't have to come from my womb to be my baby." Niecie interrupted, "I'm your baby too?" My mother smiled and said, "Yes, and you don't have to hurt anymore or be afraid anymore…" Niecie interrupted, "I ain't afraid of nobody." My mother smiled and continued, "What I'm trying to say is, we love you. I can't fix your past and I can't predict your future…no one can, but I promise you that if you give me a chance…give us a chance, we will help you get through whatever you are going through. Okay?" Niecie started to cry really hard – sobbing uncontrollably. I heard someone else crying and when I looked over at my father, I found that it was him. He wiped his eyes with one of the leaves from the bush. When he noticed that I was staring at him, he mumbled, "It's my allergies." *Yeah, right.* I thought to myself. They sat out there for another 30 minutes; this time laughing like school girls. Seeing them so happy made me happy. They stood and were walking toward us when my father and I pretended that we had lost something in the bushes. They giggled and walked passed us.

That night, when everyone was settled in, I rested in the darkness – staring at the ceiling. I couldn't fall asleep. "TKO, are you asleep?" Niecie whispered; having difficulty falling asleep too. I didn't say anything at first because I was lost in my thoughts. When I didn't answer, she turned her back to me. Pausing before speaking, I said, "What?" She turned towards me and then said, "I'm sorry for being a jerk." I didn't say anything. She continued. "I was really being stupid." I remained silent. She continued, "Did you hear me?" Breaking my silence, I said, "I was just waiting for you to get to the word that best describes you." Without saying another word, she hopped up and came over to my bed, tore away the blankets, and climbed underneath. She wrapped her arms around me and said, "I'm sorry, TKO."

Chapter 7

Teenager killed, four others wounded in South-side shooting…

TKO stood for Tijani Khalan Owens. Don't ask me what my name means or where it came from because I don't know. It was something that my mother came-up with during a drug-induced labor that lasted 12 hours. I was told that my mother had become so frustrated and angry by the time I entered the world that she told the doctor that she wanted to be the one who slapped me to make sure that I was alive. Because my name is so difficult for many people to pronounce or remember, my parents gave me the nickname, TKO. My father said that my nickname reminded him of his days on the streets. He told me that as a child, his family was poor and was always hungry. At times, he had to fight for his food – literally.

When he was young, every day after school a few kids would gather for a fight at the playground and whoever won got fifty cents. That wasn't a lot to get your teeth knocked out over, but it meant dinner to my dad who often times ate only once or twice a week. He had fought so much that he had gotten really good at it and he had to be good at it in order to survive. When he put a person down on the concrete, kids would scream, "TKO!!" Which meant that somebody got knocked out and it wasn't my daddy. I like the name because it means so much to my father.

Plus, anything was better than Tijani Khalan Owens.

I was often referred to as the "good one." Standing six feet one, I was the runt of the family. My mother, who was the shortest person in her family, stood at a mere six feet five inches and my father, who was the tallest in his family, stood at six feet seven inches. In high school, everyone thought that I would play basketball, but I wasn't interested in that. I loved music and not just any kind of music, but classical music. I loved everything about it. From Beethoven to Mozart, from the cello to the violin, I loved it, but I was ashamed of it because most folks believed that since I was young, I would naturally be drawn to rap music, but I wasn't. I don't have anything against rap music. I just don't like it. I never admitted to others that I loved classical music because I didn't want them to think that I was soft or anything. Being soft could cause teasing or even a butt-whooping and I didn't want either to happen. I would listen to it, secretively – away from the eyes and ears of others. I did that because I knew that people would tease the six foot one kid that didn't like basketball or rap music but loved the melodic sounds of Beethoven's *Fifth Symphony*. It was bad enough that I was taking honors courses in high school and everyone thought that only nerds took honors courses. The only thing that kept me from being picked on like the other kids in my class is that at 250 pounds, they thought that I would give them a run for their money.

So, I kept to myself most of the time and other than Niecie, I had no other friends. I remained to myself and that was okay. Being popular was too much work, being an athlete took too much time and energy, so being a geek was just fine for me. Who cared that I wasn't popular or that I didn't play sports. My heart belonged to music and I knew that the first opportunity to get out of this neighborhood, I was going to follow my dream of becoming a composer. I spent every hour of the day envisioning myself standing in front of millions of people, holding my baton – everyone watching me…waiting for my instruction. Conducting a piece written by Mozart with my parents in the audience would be my dream come true.

Chapter 8

An 81 years old woman was fatally shot...

One day at school, I decided not to eat lunch, but instead, I tried to find a quiet spot to listen to my music. The most secluded spot on campus was the library. When I got there, I looked around and found a spot in the back of the library away from everyone else. I was sitting on the floor, in the "M" section with my eyes closed immersed in *Mozart's Symphony No. 25 in G Minor*. Over the sound of music, I could hear people talking. I opened my eyes to see four set of legs in the next aisle. At first, I didn't think anything of it. I turned up the volume. I closed my eyes again and returned to my music.

Something told me to open my eyes and when I did, I noticed that one set of legs were dangling in the air. Suddenly, I could faintly hear someone begging and pleading, but the music was keeping me from making out what the person was saying. I removed my headphones to find someone saying, "Stop...please don't do this. I'll get your money. I promise." One of the other boys responded, "Shut up." "No," the boy begged. "Please don't...I promise, I will have your money tomorrow. I promise." Then I heard another voice say, "Look at you...sad. Why do you make me do this to you? How are we supposed to eat, if you don't bring me my money?" When he said that, I thought about the code among pimps and hoes. *You better have that damn money or suffer the consequences.*

As this went on, I could hear the music becoming louder and suddenly causing my head to hurt. As the boy pleaded, I thought about what would be the right thing to do. Every idea I came up with ended with me either getting hurt or in trouble. The boy continued to beg and after becoming impatient one of the other boys began to slap the boy. The boy screamed. "Shut-up before I shut you up…you want me to put something in your mouth to keep you quiet," the boy said. "No," the boy begged. "Then shut-up. Now, how many times am I going to have to say this? Bring me some money or get your ass kicked." Whimpering, the boy said, "I will have your money tomorrow." The other boy responded, "You will have twice as much tomorrow to make up for today." There was a pause and then the boy said, "Yes, I will try to get it." One of the other boys said, "You will try? You will try? We can't eat 'trys', so somebody better have our money or we are going to *try* not to break your ass in half." He was still dangling in the air like a helpless rag-doll.

While this went on, I sat there for a minute thinking about what to do. What would be the right thing to do? Not waiting any longer for the answer, I dropped my head, closed my eyes, removed my headphones, and then stood and walked over to where they were standing. Without thinking, I grabbed the first person that I saw and hit him so hard that I heard the bone in his jaw crack. Holding his face, he fell to the floor. I grabbed the next boy and kicked him so hard between his legs that he screamed like a girl. Looking into the direction of the boy standing in the middle of the aisle still holding the boy in the air, I said, "Drop him." He did as I told him. I shouted, "Run!" Without thinking, the boy ran, tripping over himself as he made it to the door. Now, it was three against one. We stood there looking at each other; each one waiting for someone to make the first move. All of a sudden, the bell rang. We looked at each other – staring into each other's eyes. Then we gathered our belongings. As they walked toward the door, one of them pushed me and said, "This shit ain't over."

I wasn't worried about those boys doing anything to me. They were bullies and they liked picking on kids who couldn't or wouldn't protect themselves, but I wasn't having it. If all they had were their loud mouths, I didn't have anything to worry about.

Chapter 9

Hispanic male shot, critically wounded…

When Niecie first moved in with us, she was sort of an ugly duckling – a toad in need of a magic spell and puberty was that magic spell. Niecie blossomed into the prettiest girl I've ever seen and I'm not just saying that because she's my pretend sister. I'm telling ya'…that girl is fine…I'm mean…*Sanaa Lathan* kinda fine. I'm mean, if she wasn't my sister, I would be all over 'that' "kinda fine." I have to admit that growing up together wasn't easy. When we were younger, we shared a room. At the time, it wasn't no big deal because we were kids, but when I got older, the changes in my body were becoming...noticeable and the same thing was happening to her. She had "mountains" where there were once "mole-hills" and there were parts of my body that were clearly maturing faster than I was.

The first time I noticed a change and knew what it was and why it was happening, I was scared and confused. Now, the "change" that I speak of has been happening all of my life – for as long as I can remember, but as I got older, the "change" started to mean something different to me – made me want to do things – things that, according to my mama would ensure a one-way ticket to Hell and I wasn't trying to go there.

I was feeling so awkward and weird about what was going on with my body that I decided to talk to my father about it. I thought that since he was a man too, he could tell me what to do and how to handle it, but his explanation of what was going on with my body left me more confused than ever. He looked at me and said, "Son, God made man and woman so that they can procreate. Now, when a man gets an erection…" I raised my eyebrows and then interrupted, "Ummmmmm, an erection?" I knew what an erection was, but hearing my father say the word made it sound dirty. My father looked at me and then said, "Yeah, that's what it's called boy…when your 'ding-a-ling…" I interrupted him again and said, "My ding-a-ling?" Again, I knew what it was, but hearing him say it made mine want to crawl-up inside of me. He looked at me again and then said, "…your 'man-part' boy…I

don't know what you call yours." My
eyes nearly fell out of my head. *I think
that I'm going to be sick.* "We have to
name them?" I asked. My father leaned
in and said, "Yeah, you have to give it a
name. The "man-part" is important…a
man's best friend. Yep, it will be there
for you when nobody else will. I call
mine 'The Extinguisher.'" I was
shocked, but that didn't keep me from
laughing and falling on the floor. He
smiled and continued, "Yep, yo' daddy
been putting fires out every night for the
past thirty-something years with this
thing." He had a weird look on his face
as if I should know what he was talking
about. Then suddenly, I stopped
laughing because I was reminded of the
night I walked in to him putting out one
of those "fires." I gagged. Then he
continued, "Certain things will go

through a young man's mind, and emotions will make a man want to do things with his 'ding-a-ling'…" I interrupted, "Dad, please stop calling it that. I'm begging you." He chuckled and then continued, "…that may be against God's plan, but 'man' has to be strong and resist the temptation to want to put his 'thing' into just any woman. He has to wait until God sends him the woman who will become his life-mate…put that ring on her finger and then get it on." I thought that I was going to vomit. If he continued at this rate, I was definitely going to throw up. I looked at him and then said, "Well, if God wants us to wait until He sends us our life-mate, why are these things…" I paused and pointed toward my groin and then continued, "…popping up for any woman who walks by?" My father looked at me for a minute before saying, "It's just what the body does…it is a natural response to beautiful things." Thinking, I said, "How do women hide their erection?" My father began to choke. He caught his breath, scratched his head and then said, "I've answered enough questions about this topic…and don't be no fool and go ask yo' mama how she hides an erection. That will definitely get you hurt."

One morning, I woke up and looked down to find that I wasn't the only thing ready to start the day. I tried tucking it between my legs. I tried wishing it away, but it was there to stay. While I fought with the ever-growing presence growing between my legs, Niecie walked out of the shower wearing nothing but her robe, a training bra and a matching pair of panties that my mom had brought her. Now, the 'throbbing' going on between my legs was becoming intense.

She was sitting on her bed and was rubbing lotion on her body when her robe opened slightly. I began to stare at her becoming distracted. I was looking at her so hard. First, she looked at my eyes, but then her eyes started to drift in the direction of the "unwelcome" third-party in the room. Her mouth fell open. I looked down. Now, we were both staring at it. "Boy, put that thang away," she said, pointing at my crotch. By this time, it was standing at attention –

waving back and forth like it was happy to see her. Embarrassed, I tried tucking it between my legs, but that hurt so bad, so I tried covering it with my blanket, but trying to hide it was only making it harder, so I ran into the bathroom while she laughed and teased me. "Freak!"

Hearing the commotion, my mother entered the room. "What is going on in here?" She looked around the room to find Niecie lying on her bed, laughing. She walked over to see what was going on. Through baited breath, Niecie said, "TKO has a woody." "A woody?" she asked. Wiping tears from her eyes, she pointed at the bathroom door while behind it, I was trying to hide my "manhood."

My mother knocked, but didn't wait for a response. She opened the door. When

she entered the bathroom, her mouth
fell open after finding me standing there
holding my "private-part" in my hand
trying to find somewhere to put it. For
the first time, she didn't use a Bible
scripture to fix the situation.
Embarrassed, she just covered her eyes
and ran out of the bathroom. Niecie was
still laughing. "Look at you...ran yo'
own mama out of the room with that
thing, " she said. "I hope that you choke
to death!" I shouted from the bathroom.
The next day, I had my own bedroom.

Chapter 10

Man fatally shot in Chicago Heights…

A fter that "event", we became
uncomfortable around each
other. I would never admit this
to anyone, but looking at Niecie made
me feel things that a brother should
never feel for his sister – pretend or not.
Even though she wasn't my "blood,"
she was still my sister. I grew up with
her. We slept in the same bed together.
We went to church together. We were
raised by the same woman who taught
us the "birds and the bees" and in that
conversation she was very thorough
about what was and what was not
acceptable sexual behavior. And
although, she didn't mention it, I'm sure

that me wanting to get my freak on with my "sister" was a "no-no."

I couldn't understand why I was feeling that way and late at night when I'm was alone, I couldn't stop thinking about her - how grown-up she is. My sister is sexy and I dare not say that out-loud, but everything she did was so….sexual. I can't explain it. The way she laughed, the way that she curled-up like a ball on the sofa to watch television, and the way that she ate cereal…Man, I can't explain it, but after watching her eat a bowl of cereal, I had to run and take a cold shower.

One day, we were wrestling like we used to when we were little and ended-up on top of each other. For a moment, we just laid there – staring into each other's eyes. With our bodies pressed against each other, I could feel her heartbeat racing underneath her V-neck sweater. I could tell that she wanted to kiss me and believe me, I wanted to kiss her too, but I couldn't, so I stared at her lips and imagined how sweet they were. The image sent chills through my body. I wanted to touch her, but kept my hands to my side. Although it felt so right, I knew that it was wrong. I began to feel that throbbing sensation, again, between my legs. My body became rigid, but not in a good way. I tried shifting my body so that she couldn't feel the growing presence between my legs, but no matter how hard I tried to, my body wanted her. I knew that if I remained there any longer something was going to happen because we both wanted it to and even though I could probably name a hundred reasons why it would be okay, I had one good reason why it wasn't. She was my sister.

I looked at her one last time, and then closed my eyes and turned my head looking away from her. She pulled at my face, but I used everything in me not to give in – to become weak and do something that I would regret for the rest of my life. When she realized that I wouldn't succumb to the intensity of the moment, she let me face go, and whispered in my ear, "I love you too."

I had to talk to my father about this
because I felt so guilty and confused.
When I got home from school, I found
him resting in his recliner and watching
television. When I approached him, I
hesitated, became afraid, and decided
that this topic was too embarrassing to
talk about. I turned to leave the room
when I heard him say, "Hey son, what's
going on?"

"Ummmmmm, nothing dad...go back to
what you were doing?" He sat up in his
chair. "Come on son...you look troubled.
What's going on?" I dropped my head,
took a deep breath and then said,

"Something is bothering me, dad, but...it's complicated."

He grabbed the remote, turned down the volume down on the television and then said, "Would you like to pray first?"

"No," I said. "It's hard enough to have to talk about it, but to pray before I say it...that's too weird...again, this is too complicated." "Look son...nothing is too weird or complicated for God." I scratched my head and then said, "I was kinda hoping that I could just talk to you...and leave Him out of it." Shocked, he said, "Leave God out of it??? If God can't be in it then neither should you."

His words struck a chord. I looked up at him and then smiled. That was the answer that I was looking for. "You're right, dad...thank you so much."

Now, scratching his head, my father said, "Ummmmm....okay...glad that I could help."

I smiled, kissed him on the forehead, and then said, "Yep, dad, you always have the best answer."

He smiled and then said, "Sure son...anytime."

We both smiled at each other before I walked out of the room. On the way out, I thought about what he said and he was right. If what I was doing or thinking about doing was going to cause me to leave God out of it then I shouldn't be involved in it. If He couldn't be involved in the choices that I

make throughout my life then I was
making the wrong choices.

Chapter 11

An eight year old, was fatally shot while sitting in the living room of her mother's home...

I was raised in the church. As a small child, I didn't like attending service, but as I got older, I began to really like it. I loved attending service because being there gave me a sense of peace that the external world couldn't provide. I loved listening to the music and I loved how no matter what was going on in the "real world", on Sunday morning, nothing else mattered.

It was interesting because I knew most of these people and in the real world, they led very…very different and interesting lives.

For instance, Mrs. Baker. Mrs. Baker is one of the ushers. She has been a member of the church for at least 10 years. Now, Mrs. Baker looks like a Godly woman, but when she's not at church, I know for a fact that she frequents an afterhours club near my home and I'm not saying that there's anything wrong with that, because she might be going there to help show those people the 'err of their ways' - help save their souls, but I don't know how she's saving them from the backseat of their car.

Every night Mrs. Baker is seen leaving with a different man and every night, she is seen butt-naked doing Lawd-knows what in somebody's car.

One night, my mom and I were walking back from the grocery store and walked passed a car that was rocking back and forth. The windows were fogged up and there was so much noise coming from inside that it caused us to stop and look in. When we approached it, we found Mrs. Baker in the back seat - legs all up in the air. I tried to see more, but my mother pulled my arm and then told me to come on. "You don't want to see that mess. That's between her and God. God is gonna take care of that, amen?" I looked at her and then said, "But right now, somebody else is taking care of 'that'...amen?" She didn't like that response, because after I said it she smacked me in the back of the head.

And poor Mr. Baker. He sat on the Deacon's Board. Every night, you could find him at the liquor store. Now, I'm not saying that drinking is wrong because they drank wine in the Bible, but the amount of liquor that Mr. Baker drank was clearly a sin. Anytime you drink to the point that you can't find your way home - you walk up and down the street flashing people while singing church songs; something is seriously wrong. But the Bakers are no different than most of the folks in the church. I call those folks, Sunday Morning Christians, because they sinned Monday thru Saturday and come to church on Sunday morning and sit in those pews like little angels. They come to be saved - to find salvation after they have done all sorts of sinful things during the week, but no one's perfect and that's the cool thing about church; every Sunday, you could find your

imperfect-self surrounded by more
imperfect people.

Chapter 12

A little girl was shot in the Roseland area…

T oday, had something great in store for me. I could feel it. There was something special about today. From the moment that I woke up, I knew it. Everything about "today" was perfect – perfect weather, I woke-up at a perfect time, ate a perfect breakfast, took a shower, got dressed, picked out a perfect outfit to wear, and looked in the mirror. Damn, I looked perfect in it. I couldn't wait to get to service. All the way to church, I keeping thinking to myself how lucky it was to be so blessed – to know that God loved me. It was such an incredible feeling.

When I walked in, there were so many people there that they were being herded like sheep from one door to another. Since I had a few minutes before service started, I decided to stop to get a cup of tea from the Starbuck's Kiosk. As I sipped from my cup of tea, I decided to check-out the books in the church's bookstore. I searched the shelves to find a beautiful brown-leathered-bound Bible with gold trim. I set my cup down to inspect the pages. *This would make a beautiful gift for my mother,* I thought to myself as I scrolled through the pages. As I held the book, a voice from across the room, said, "Should I ring that up for you?" Startled, I looked in the direction of the voice. There was a young girl sitting behind the counter. I don't know how I missed her when I walked in, but there she was – cute, odd, but cute. She was petite, about 4'11", short-cropped hair, big brown eyes that sat behind the thickest pair of glasses I've ever seen. Looking at her, I could only think of all of the cruel jokes that I've once said about people who wore thick glasses. One joke was, "Your glasses are so thick that you could look at a map and see people waving." I used to love that joke, until now, for some odd reason it didn't seem that funny. I placed the book down, grabbed my cup of tea, and was walking toward the counter when I saw the lit sign in the hallway indicating that service was starting. Before leaving the store, I introduced myself to the young lady. I smiled and extended my hand. "Hi…I'm TKO." Before accepting my hand, she smiled back. "TKO??? Isn't that the title of a song?" I paused before responding. She wore braces and the amount of metal in her mouth was distracting. There was so much steel in her mouth, her head alone weigh 40 pounds. Her smile must have been really torn-up that someone felt that she needed that much metal in her mouth. She could set-off every metal detector from here to Africa, but that didn't matter though, because she was still cute.

Shaking from my trance, I responded to her question. "What? Yeah, that's my name…I mean, that's my nickname. My real name is Tijani Khalan Owens." "Tijani," she purred. When she said my name, I smiled. I wanted to hear her say it again, so I pretended that I didn't hear her. I said, "What?" Then she said it again, "Tijani." *Sweet.* I thought to myself. I could have stood there and listened to her repeat it over-and-over again all day. I was staring at her, when she said, "My name is, Toni…with an 'i'." "Toni," I repeated. "I like that." I was still holding out my hand. Suddenly I realized how long I had been holding it there and she did too. She then apologized. "I'm so sorry." She took my hand. Her hands were smooth like the skin of a new born. I was caught-up in her smile, when she cleared her throat. "Ummmm…???" She looked down at her hand; the hand that I was still holding and didn't want to let go. Shaking me loose, I said, "I better go." She smiled and said,

"Sure…maybe, I'll see you later." Walking toward the door, I said, "Sure." I was halfway in the hallway when she approached me, from behind, touching me on the shoulder. "You forgot your tea." I took the cup from her hand, making sure that I touched it again. "Thank you," I said and smiled. She turned to walk away, but looked over her shoulder to find that I was staring at her. When she noticed it, she began to move her hips in such a way that they looked like palm trees that were swaying in the wind. I watched her butt move back-and-forth until she was completely out of sight.

I had to clear my head before going inside because what I wanted to do to her, at that moment, was definitely a sin. I had to make sure that I asked for forgiveness when I got inside, but until then, I couldn't shake what I was feeling. So much so, that when I entered the room, I grabbed a seat in the corner, so that I could fantasize about her out of the view of the eyes of the statue of Jesus that sat on the altar.

They turned the lights off and turned on the big screen TVs to read the announcements. There was an announcement indicating that the church would be hosting a NBA Championship Game party and that all were invited. I was making a mental note of the event when a person came over and sat next to me. It was Toni. I smiled. I was so excited that my hands began to sweat. I wasn't expecting this, so my plans to fantasize about her were squashed. The real thing was sitting next to me. This day couldn't get any better.

She remained seated next to me for the entire service. We talked about everything. Her family, her favorite hobbies, her likes, and her dislikes. By the time the service was over, I knew almost everything about her. The entire time she spoke, I could only image how good she would look if she didn't have to wear those glasses and those braces.

She said something funny. I don't know what she said, but it was clearly funny to her. Watching her laugh made me laugh. We both laughed so loud that the people in front of us shushed us. We giggled and quieted long enough to pay our "tithes and offering." Shortly after, the pastor dismissed the congregation and we all poured into the hall. Looking at her, told me why today would be so perfect – I was supposed to meet her.

We were walking towards the door, when someone called her name. She turned and began to wave. She looked at me. "That's my mom and dad…you don't mind sticking around to meet them, do you?" I began to feel uncomfortable. "Your parents? Isn't it too soon?" She twisted-up the corner of her mouth. "Are you serious? Boy, stop playing." She hit me in the arm. "It ain't like we're getting married or anything…I just love my parents and I want you to meet them." Grabbing my arm, I said, "Sure." When her parents approached us, she said, "Mom and dad, I want you to meet my new friend, Tijani. Tijani, this is my mom and dad." I extended my hand and then said, "It is so nice to meet you both." Without saying anything, her father took my hand, he held it, firmly – *a little tighter than necessary*, I thought to myself. "It's nice to meet you too," her mother said pulling on her husband's arm so that he could release his grip. I shook my hand to relieve the pain and without smiling, I looked at him – we looked each other. His look made it clear that he wasn't taking no mess when it came to his daughter and my look meant that I couldn't agree more.

We were all leaving the building and talking when we heard a popping sound coming from across the street. We all looked in its direction. Suddenly, a young man came out of nowhere and landed at the foot of the church's steps. "Help me," he said. He reached out to us, but no one moved. We all stood there and looked at him. Before I knew it, without thinking, I was running toward him. When I got to him, out of the blue, another male walked up, with a gun in his hand, he stood in front of me. I stopped. *Frozen*. I couldn't think. The young man looked me straight in the eyes. I stared back. As we stood there looking at each other, I could hear the young man whimpering, "Please help me. Don't let him kill me." I didn't want to move because I was afraid of what he might do, so I kept my eyes on him. This went on for what seemed like forever. *He's going to kill me. Keep your cool or he will shoot you.* I thought as I stood there. Something in my eyes must have indicated that we had an understanding, because he didn't shoot me. Satisfied with what he saw on my face, the young man smiled out of the corner of his mouth. He turned to walk away, but before leaving, he walked over to the young man lying on the steps and standing over him, he pulled the trigger once more (Pop!) and then he ran away.

It all seemed so unreal to me. It was like I was watching a movie. For at least ten minutes, I stood there without moving – in complete shock. When I finally realized what was happening, I looked down in the direction of where the body lay. At first I didn't see his body just the blood as it poured down the stairs. Still in shock, I walked over and kneeled down beside him and grabbed his hand. With his eyes wide open, he looked at me. I looked at him. He didn't say anything. He just looked blankly in my direction. I looked up at the doors of the church to find people watching and whispering as he took his last breaths. Finally, the pastor emerged from the crowd to instruct everyone to return inside. As people retreated back into the church, I turned my attention back to the young man whose chest expanded one last time and then there was nothing. His body went limp and his hand began to feel heavy as I held it. I wanted to cry, but I couldn't. I just sat there until the police arrived.

When they arrived, they brought the media with them. At this time, everyone had gathered outside close to where the body lay. As I looked at the blood on my hands, I continued to try to make sense of the whole event. Toni was trying to get me to leave the body, but I didn't move until the police had instructed me to do so and even then, I didn't want to. I felt like it was my duty to be there for the young man until someone came to help him, and for some really odd reason, I felt like I needed to protect him.

The pastor and his wife were "primping" for their on-the-spot-camera interview. "How do I look?" asked the pastor. He adjusted the jacket of what looked like a very expensive suit and fixed the tie and the collar of what looked like a very expensive shirt. "You look fine. How do I look?" asked the First Lady, who was dressed to the "nines" herself. "You look fine," the pastor confirmed. The cameras started rolling, and instead of interviewing the pastor and his wife, the reporter walked up to me. Before I could decline making a comment, they had the microphone in my face. "Did you get a chance to see the face of the person who did this?" Her question triggered the memory of me and the gunman, face-to-face. The memory caused tears to develop in my eyes. I looked at her with the straightest look on my face, I paused and then said, "I didn't see anything." When the words came out of my mouth it was like my brain had completely shut-down and without any control of my own, I lied. *I lied.* I knew that I saw the face of the killer. I would never forget his face even if I wanted to, but there I stood lying on the steps of the Lord's house. I was so ashamed and before the reporter could ask me another question, I walked away with my head bowed down.

A police officer approached me. Stopping me, he said, "I know that you saw something and I know that you're scared, but…"He placed his hand on my shoulder and then continued, "When you're ready to talk…" He was handing me his card when I said, "I didn't see anything. Now, I have to go home." The police officer stuck the card into my face. "Take this…if you want to talk." I looked at him, took the card, placed it into my pocket, and started to walk away. "Tijani! Tijani!" I heard Toni's voice calling me from a distance. I kept walking and didn't look back. I didn't want to talk to her. Her voice became a part of a memory that I would spend the rest of my life trying to erase.

The

Meantime...

Chapter 13

Three men were wounded in a drive-by shooting…

I couldn't fall asleep. Believe me, I tried, but I couldn't. Every time, I closed my eyes, I could see the young man lying on the concrete, looking at me with pleading eyes - my reflection, in them, staring back at me. Two bullet wounds, that's all it took and then he was gone – just like that.

Questions began to clutter my mind. I tossed and turned as the questions bombarded my thoughts. I tried to imagine what he was thinking as he took his last breath. I wondered what events led up to that moment. I

wondered what his morning was like.
Did he know that he was going to die or
did he wake up and do the same things
I did? Did we both wake up with the
Lord on our minds? Was he getting
ready for church and on his way there
when something happened? Did he go
left when he should have gone right?
He woke up when he should have slept-
in? He wore the wrong colors, walked
down the wrong street, waved the left
hand in a neighborhood where they
only waved their right hands? Was he
on the wrong street corner trying to
cross the street and somebody wanted
to teach him a lesson about the rules of
the road and things got out of hand?
What did he do that was so wrong that
somebody felt that the only punishment
for his behavior or lack thereof was
death? What? What? What? I wanted to

know. I had to know why someone decided that he had to die. I wanted to know what could he have done that could have caused someone else to decide that he was unworthy of life and why? Also, I wasn't the only person who witnessed the crime. Why didn't anyone else speak up? Out of all of the questions that I had, that one, I knew the answer to - for the same reason that I didn't say anything - because we were afraid.

Then I thought about myself and how close I came to being killed. There, the killer and I stood, face-to-face, with a gun in his hand. He could have pulled the trigger and ended my life, but there was something in letting me live that pleased him. He smiled like he knew something that I didn't know. Whatever it was, I was grateful that he didn't shoot me. I'm sure that he had some bullets left for the person that he knew could finger him or maybe he knew that I wouldn't say anything and why waste a bullet on a coward. As I sat there thinking about the whole situation, I remembered the look on everyone's face as the young man lie helpless on the steps of the church. I thought about how the pastor shielded the congregation to protect them, but after watching how they "primped" for the cameras, I couldn't help but wonder if they were trying to protect their congregation or the weekly salary that paid for their fancy wardrobe, their fancy cars, or for that big beautiful home that they lived in. Something about them and the whole situation made me sick to my stomach.

Then I thought about me and how ashamed I felt at that moment; as they drew a chalk-line around his body, and how I lied to the media, the police officer, and to every person who would see the news that night. As his life became nothing more to the world than another blurb in the news, another Black man shot dead in the hood, I lied. I didn't even value his life enough to tell the truth about what happened to him. Because in all truth…in all truth…I didn't care about him…I couldn't have…just like all of those people who stood twenty feet away and watched him die. Caring would have included more than my sympathy – I should have told the police who killed him.

"Don't be a tattle-tale", a lesson that I learned as a child, quickly became,

"Don't be a snitch" as I got older. You just didn't do it, so instinctively I lied because that's what I was told to do in moments like these. From the moment that I was old enough to understand, my parents taught me the ABCs of the streets and how to survive being a young male growing up in Chicago. There were a lot of rules and they were always changing, but there was one rule that stayed the same. Mind your own business and never snitch. *Well, one out of two ain't bad.* I remember the day that they explained it to me. I could hear my parents now. I remember the conversation as if we had it just this morning:

"If it ain't none of your business, you keep it moving," my mother said. My father confirmed this by saying, "What good

would it do to get shot or caught-up over somebody else's mess. I don't want to get no phone call telling me that you got shot in the butt because you didn't know when to mind your own business or you got shot trying to defend somebody and then what? There are a lot of heroes in the ground and in Heaven that ended-up there too soon." My mother piggy-backed on his comments by saying, "We don't want to lose our baby like that."

I responded. "Ain't they somebody's baby too?" My parents paused and then looked at each other. My father broke the silence by saying, "Yes, they are somebody's baby, but they are not our baby. They are somebody else's baby and somebody's else's problem. We have enough to deal with. We can't be running around here trying to save everybody. Now, do as you're told. Go to bed, so that you can get ready for Sunday *school in the morning and don't forget what I said…keep your mouth closed." "Okay dad," I said before leaving the room. Thinking I asked them both this question. "Mom…dad…what would Jesus do?" My father looked at me and then said, "When they hung Jesus on the cross among those thieves do you think somebody did all they could to stop them from killing Him? The Bible tells you that folks stood and looked while others mocked Him. The only person that said something was one of the criminals who were being killed too. A couple of folks may have said or tried to do something, but I bet that they were punished for it and He was still crucified. Evil people don't care and Jesus Christ was the son of God. Folks didn't stand up for Him. They could have, but they didn't…at least not enough to keep Him from dying, so what makes you think these folks 'round here is gon' stick their neck out* for one of these little kids? Please...all of this killing would stop if folks opened their mouths, but they are scared and they should be. These folks are walking around with guns killing any and everybody, and for what? Nothing...if they don't care about shooting a baby...a little kid...six or seven years old...sitting on the porch minding their own business then what do you think that they would do to a snitch? If they cared about anybody other than themselves, they would stop, but they don't. They will kill you no matter what...no matter if you're good or bad. Those bullets don't care who they come in contact with. It's just another child gon'. Now, I'm done talking about this. You keep your mouth closed...and go to bed!"

I laid there hoping that sleep would embrace me soon, but it didn't happen. My family had gone to bed hours earlier and I was left lying awake alone to deal with the tragedy of the day. I was staring at the ceiling when I heard a loud noise come from down the hall. At first, I shook it off until I heard it again. This time I stood to leave the room, but not before retrieving my bat from under the bed. I was walking down the hall when I heard the sound again, this time coming from Niecie's room. When I entered, I turned on the light to find her crawling inside of the window. I looked at her, turned the light off and walked out of her room. She came running after me, but I didn't stop. "TKO, stop…where are you going? You're not going to tell mom and dad are you?" I didn't respond and kept walking. Trying to explain herself, she said, "Look… me and a few of my friends were just hanging out…that's all." I flipped around to face her. "Really?" I scowled. "That's all you were doing was hanging out? You don't watch the freakin' news…folks are getting shot…News Flash! And they are dying too and why? Because they were just hanging out." I was walking away when she folded her arms and said, "Are you serious?" Frowning, she continued, "I won't say what I'm thinking because I think that you're suffering from some form of mental breakdown, so I'm going to be easy on you….but for the record, most of the people who are hanging out don't expect to get shot. If they did, I'm sure that they would do everything to avoid getting shot...dummy. Folks don't just wake-up and say, 'Hey, I think I want to hang out and get shot today.' Somebody decides it for them. You think some six year old child, who is playing in front of their house wants to get shot? You have some special stuff going on if you think that is what people want to happen to them. We would like to think that we're safe." "But you're not safe..." I shouted and then continued, "We're not safe..." She looked at me and then unfolded her arms. "No one wants to die. We want to live without worrying about dying."

I looked at her and then turned to walk away. She grabbed my arm, "'T', don't you hear me talking to you?" I pulled away and then blurted, "I saw a boy get shot today and while I'm trying to understand all of this, you drag your stupid butt in here in the middle of the night like some..." I paused and looked her up and down. I frowned. I couldn't believe what she was wearing. I continued, "...like some hood-rat...like it ain't nothing going on around you...folks are dying and you are out there acting fast. You know better and just like half the folks that end-up with a bullet in their butts, you seem to think that your ass is bullet-proof." Niecie looked at me and said, "What did you call me? I KNOW you didn't call me no hood-rat. Since it looks like you are going through some things, I'm going to give you a pass." I looked at her and then said, "A pass on what? I almost got shot today...another person was killed…don't threaten me little girl. I ain't even in the mood." Shaking my head, I continued, "Do you really think I care right now about what you're talking about?"

She put her hand on her hip and was about to say something, but stopped and said, "What? You almost got shot?" I looked at her. Now, I just told her that someone got killed and I ALMOST got shot and she looked right over the fact that someone was killed. I just shook my head and began to walk toward the room. She followed closely behind me. "What happened? Are you okay?" "Yeah, I'm fine, but the other person isn't." "Wow…I'm glad that you're okay." Again, she looked right over the fact that someone else actually got shot and died today. "Niecie, did you hear me? I said that I ALMOST got shot, but somebody else, actually, got shot right in front of me...and died." She looked at me for a moment as if she was trying to process what I was saying and then she said, "That's kinda messed-up..." "Kinda messed-up? Kinda...? Are you serious? A boy lost his life today. Why is it taking so long for you to get this? Are you smoking some of that stuff?" She shook her head and said, "Naw man'...it's just...it's just...that I don't know him and..." I interrupted her. "SO you have to know a person to feel something for them? Damn, that's cold. This world is so messed up." She said, "Why do you say that? I mean...I care, but that stuff happens all of the time around here. Hearing about a child being shot in Chicago is so common... it's like asking somebody what is today's date?" And why do you care? It wasn't you." I frowned and said, "But it could have been. The killer was standing right in my face…holding a gun." She had a surprised look on her face. "You saw the killer?" Becoming agitated, I said, "Didn't I say that I almost got shot?" She responded. "Yeah, but you didn't say that the killer was standing in your face." Shaking her head, she continued, "Wow…what are you going to do?" Rubbing my head, I said, "I'm going to try to do what I've been trying to do all day…I'm going to stop thinking about it by not talking about it." She looked at me and then said, "That's not going to make it go away." I sighed. "I know," I said, before turning the lights out.

Chapter 14

49 year old stabbed to death in the
Englewood neighborhood…

The next morning, I awoke to my mom and dad standing over me and staring. When I tried to stretch, I felt something at the foot of my bed. It was Niecie. I kicked her and when she looked up, I pointed in their direction. We were wiping sleep from our eyes, when dad said, "You have to get ready for school. Let's go."

Still half asleep, we got up and did what we were told. Niecie and I went our separate ways while dad and mom walked downstairs toward the kitchen. I walked over to my closet to find

something to wear, but I couldn't think
– couldn't concentrate on what I was
doing. Just seventeen hours earlier, I
saw someone get killed. How do you
move on from that? How do you just go
on with your life after someone else's
life had been taken? I just couldn't do it.
A wave of depression fell over me. I
walked over to my bed and climbed
underneath my blankets, wrapping the
blankets around my head, I tried to go
back to sleep.

A few minutes later, my mom entered
the room. "Okay, let's go…you have
things to do and people to see." I
moaned displaying my dissatisfaction
with her request. Becoming impatient,
she walked over to the bed and tried to
pull the blankets off of me, but I
wouldn't let go. She played Tug-of-War

with me for about a minute, then I let go
of the blankets and she went flying
across the room, hitting the floor. I
jumped-up and then ran to help her. I
reached for her to help her to her feet.
When I stuck out my hand, I couldn't
help but remember the young man who
got shot. I pulled my hand back causing
her to fall back again; hitting the floor.
"Boy!" she shouted. I stared at her with
a blank look on my face. She shouted
again, "Boy, will you give me a hand?" I
walked away, grasping my head into
my hands. As she struggled to get up
she said, "What is wrong with you?"
She dusted her clothing as she walked
toward me. I didn't hesitate to tell her. I
didn't even care that she would end-up
getting mad at me. I had to get this off
of my chest. I had to tell somebody.

"Yesterday, at service, a boy got shot and…" She interrupted me, "A boy got shot…at church…a boy…got shot?" She sat and looked at me in disbelief. I tried to continue, but she interrupted me again, "A boy got shot…at the church?" "Yes," I answered. She paused and then said, "Nothing happened to the Pastor and the First Lady, did it?" I couldn't believe her. Sarcastically, I responded, "Nooooo…no one as important as them. Naw, it was just some regular person." She had a blank look on her face indicating that she missed the sarcasm. Looking at her, I continued, "No, now like I was saying…a boy got shot and I was trying to help him when the boy who shot him walked up to me and…" She began to choke, trying to speak, because her words wouldn't come out fast enough. "What the hell are you talking about?!!!" "I was trying to tell you that…," I responded. I tried to finish the story, when she stood and walked over to the door and yelled, "Daddy, could you come in here for a minute?" She slammed the door closed and then reopened it and then shouted, "Bring me some aspirin and a glass of wine!" When my dad entered the room, she immediately grabbed the contents from his hand and in one big gulp everything was gone. She held the glass to her mouth, patting the back of it as if there was more in it. "Why didn't you bring the whole bottle up here?" she asked. Looking confused, he said, "What's going on?" Pacing back and forth, she paused and said, "YOUR child was just telling me about a shooting at the church that he was involved in." It was amazing how in times when I did good, I was her child, but when I did something stupid, I was his child. I stood and then said, "Come on now, ma'…that's not what I said." With his eyes squinting, my father said, "Are you talking back to her? I KNOW YOU AIN'T TALKING BACK." He began to roll up his sleeves. I put my hands together and then said, "Time-out…I'm trying to tell you something." "Well, you need to talk faster," my mother said, still pacing the floor. "Yeah, talk faster," my father repeated. Before, I opened my mouth, my mother said, "The one day that we decide to stay home…a boy gets shot. I told you that we should have went to the morning service, but noooooooo, you wanted to wait until after your game." My father looked at my mother and then said, "I know you not trying to blame something on me…we would have made the morning service if you weren't running around trying to get your freak on until the wee hours of the morning." We heard laughter coming from the hall. My mother walked over to the door to find Niecie bent over and laughing so hard, she was crying. Holding her stomach and laughing, she said, "Y'all still do the freaky-deaky…at your age?" She wiped tears from her eyes, and continued, "Church-folks get down like that…what? Who would have thought?" She continued to laugh. My mother was growing impatient. "Girl, get your butt up and get in here," she said, angrily. "What do you know about this?" While all of this was going on, I had my hand in the air like I was at school trying to get my teacher's attention. "Ummmmmm??? Can I finish telling you what happened?" The room fell silent. It was weird. I didn't know what to do at first, so I didn't say anything. Everyone was looking in my direction. "Oh…okay…like I was saying," I began. "I was at church. We were leaving when we heard a popping sound…suddenly, a boy appeared out of nowhere…fell on the church's steps…blood was everywhere…"As I spoke, I could see his face – the look in his eyes as he cried for help. I continued. "I ran to help him…" My father interrupted me. "You did what? Boy, what the hell did I tell you about that? DIDN'T I TELL YOU TO MIND YOUR OWN BUSINESS?" WHAT PART OF MINDING YOUR OWN BUSINESS IS A PROBLEM FOR YOU???" He paused and waited for an answer. I opened my mouth to speak when he interrupted and said, "Well??? I'm waiting." I was about to answer again, when my mother interrupted. "He's hard-headed...when he ends-up with a bullet in his ass we won't have to tell him to mind his own business." Angrily, my father blurted out, "Snitches are bitches who end-up in ditches!" The entire room fell quiet. We were all stunned. No one said anything – trying to absorb what he said. He broke the silence. "Well, it's the truth." *Church folk*, I thought to myself.

I became frustrated. I couldn't take it anymore. I spoke without waiting for them to interrupt me again. "I did what those church folks should have been doing. How could I stand by and watch that boy lay there, dying? I couldn't and I didn't care that the boy who shot him was there...I..." This time Niecie interrupted, "The boy who shot him was there? You saw him?" She said that like she had just heard it for the first time, but I knew what she was doing. She was trying to act like she didn't know anything, so when the punishment was handed out she wouldn't get served. I sneered in her direction. My mother and father were shaking their heads and mumbling under their breaths.

"Yes, he was there and you know what? I didn't care." Shaking her head, my mother spoke. "Boy, you have lost your mind. Are you smoking those funny cigarettes?" Frowning, I said, "Funny cigarettes??? What are you talking about???" Niecie started laughing again. "Funny cigarettes…that's funny." We all looked in her direction. She threw her hand in the air to surrender. My father began to look around the room for something. When he couldn't find it, he said, "What does the Bible say about being disobedient?" My mother looked at him with a blank look on her face. She knew the answer, but she didn't want to show him up, so we all waited until he found it himself. He said, "A hard head makes a soft behind…" "I don't think that's in there," my mother said. "And what does that mean, anyway?" Niecie said. My father gave them both a look that stopped any additional comments from being said.

Niecie said, "Okay…okay…okay…continue…I won't say nothing else." I responded. "Yes, I ran out there. I didn't think about it. I just did it and I can't say that thinking about it would have changed anything. He was dying and he needed my help." My mother threw her hands in the air and looking at the ceiling, she said, "Lord, please help this child…something is wrong with him." Turning to me, she continued, "You could have been killed." I replied. "I could have, but I wasn't. It's funny…I would have expected a different response from you guys being Christians and all." My father sounded off first. "Who the fuc…?" He stopped, looked around the room at the shocked faces, took a deep breath and then continued, "Boy…you just don't know." He put his hands on his hips and began to walk back and forth, while shaking his head. We all sat quietly, waiting for his response. Taking a deep breath he said, "I know why you did it son. You wanted to do the right thing in a world

that often encourages the wrong thing. I
know what you were trying to do, but
you shouldn't have done that."

I interrupted him, "How is it that so
many folks believe in God, but fear the
Devil. If we believe the stuff that we've
been taught then we shouldn't fear
anyone or anything because the Bible
says, "'Yea, though I walk through the
valley of the shadow of death, I will fear
no evil: for thou art with me; thy rod
and thy staff they comfort me.' We learn
it and recite it like a lyric to a song
instead of something to live by, so while
people are being gunned down in the
streets, we turn our heads, close our
blinds, and our mouths like a bunch of
cowards…like a bunch of hypocrites.
You should have seen all of those folks
run in the other direction like that was

the best answer. They only came out when the policed showed-up. I couldn't have been the only person who saw the killer's face, but they didn't say or do anything..." Niecie looked at me. "You were there when the police showed-up right?" Shaking my head, I said, "Shut up, you know I was." Mom and dad turned to look at her. She didn't care that they were looking at her. She looked like she was having a lot of fun. With her head titled to the side, she said, "So you told them who did it?" I dropped my head into my hands and began to shake my head. "No," I said, regrettably. She continued. "So you didn't do no more than the folks you're criticizing right now...so... uummmm...who's the hypocrite?" I stood and walked over to her. I stared at her. I wanted to hit her, but I didn't.

She was right and hitting her wasn't going to make her wrong. Defeated and feeling disgusted with myself, I walked out of the room. "Tijani, get back here...right now! We are not done talking to you!" My mother yelled. I heard my father say, "Mama, let him go. He has to figure this one out on his own."

Chapter 15

26 year old White male shot in McKinley Park...

I had to get out of there. If I had sat there any longer, I was going to scream. There they were judging me and I knew that what I did was right. But it wasn't enough. I should have said something. Niecie was right. I was no better than the people who ran back in that church hiding from the truth – people are being shot and killed and no one cares but the families who are left behind to mourn and bury their loved ones. How can I call myself a man while I stand back and lie to protect the people killing their children? Then I thought about it. *A man has no fear. He*

stands up for what he believes in. A man
protects his community and fights for
what's right and against what's wrong.
Then I remembered the look on the
killer's face. He wasn't afraid. He wasn't
scared of me or the people in the church
and it wasn't because he had a gun. No,
it was something else. I've seen it before
– in Brenda's eyes. That void. That
emptiness. He had no soul like a dead
person. He wasn't afraid of death;
giving it or receiving it because he was
already dead inside. To kill another
human being is cold-hearted and only
dead people have cold hearts. But how
does a person get that way? Abuse?
Neglect? Hate? What? I'll never
understand it.

I just started walking to 'nowhere' – thinking about my family and when walking began to take too long to get me to 'nowhere,' I started to run and I kept running until my feet became too sore and too heavy to take another step. I was standing in front of a drug store when I stopped. Out of breath, I began to look around. Everywhere I looked, there was someone standing on the street. It was 9am and people were in the streets instead of at work or at school.

Young girls who were dressed provocatively were laughing, talking loudly, and cursing, while the men looked on like hungry dogs waiting to attack their prey. There were young girls pushing strollers with babies in them. The young men, with their pants hanging off of their backsides, touched the young girls as they laughed and giggled with acceptance. There was music blaring from the window of a car sitting on the corner while drugs exchanged hands. An old woman tried walking pass a group of young people who were hogging the sidewalk. No one moved so that she could pass. They just became louder.

When I looked at the buildings on the opposite side of the street, things didn't look any better. The buildings that occupied the street were a church…a barber shop…a liquor store…a beauty supply store…a hair salon…a Mickey

D's…an abandoned house…another liquor store…and finally, another church and right across the street is this…madness. I couldn't believe my eyes. I have walked down this street at least a million times, but for the first time, I saw it – the disease that was killing our people. No one cared anymore.

As I stood there, looking around, a car drove by. The closer it got the slower the speed as it approached. I looked into the window at its occupants and there he was – the killer – the murderer – smiling at me.

There we were again, looking at each other. I didn't say anything and neither did he. He winked at me and then pulled off. I watched as the car rolled down the street.

Chapter 16

People take to the streets to march against the senseless violence in Chicago...

T he next day...

"Tijani...Tijani...," the teacher called. She walked over to my desk and leaned over until we were looking each other in the eye. "Tijani??? Are you with me???" I snapped out of my trance. "Ummmm, yeah, sure...I'm with you." Smiling, she said, "We were discussing the Transatlantic Slave Trade and the Black Holocaust. Would you like to add to the discussion?" Flipping through the pages of my English book, I said, "Yeah sure...let me see..." She looked at me and then said, "If you were paying attention, you would know that you're not in your English class, but in History...now, can you add something to the discussion?" I thought for a minute before answering. "The Slave Trade and the Black Holocaust..." I thought back again to the young man who was killed and then said, "Black people are enslaved mentally, physically, financially, and emotionally on a day-to-day basis. Yes, we were enslaved and brought here unwillingly and in many cases, deceived by our own people – killed, raped, shackled, mutilated, and lynched – bound by our hands and feet, our voices were silenced for fear of retaliation from those who enslaved us. As people were being killed and raped, we closed our mouths and looked away. The "masters" would

force us to watch as they destroyed us –
our minds and our bodies and
threatened to kill us if we spoke up or
against them. Now, we do the same
thing…as people are gunned down in
our streets – the streets where the
houses sit that we call our homes - we
look away as we've been trained to do
our entire lives and the Black Holocaust
may have happened many years ago,
but look around you…it is happening
right here and right now…right in front
of us. This is GENOCIDE!" I shouted
and then slammed my hand on the
desk. The whole classroom fell silent.
No one said anything. They just stared
at me. Even the teacher stared. Everyone
was speechless. Then the bell rang. As
we all stood to leave the room, the
teacher stopped me. "Mr. Owens…is
everything okay?" I looked at her. "No,

it's not." I turned and walked out of the classroom.

In the hall, I was putting my books into my locker when I heard a familiar voice call my name. "Tijani! Tijani!" I looked up to find Toni running towards me. Initially, I hesitated. I couldn't help but see that young man's face as she said my name, but it was something about her that made me want to think only about her – forget about the madness. I couldn't help, but smile. Something about her just made everything seem okay; at least for the moment. When she approached me, without saying another word, she stood on her toes, wrapped her arms around my shoulders and hugged me tightly – almost made me drop my books on the floor. She whispered in my ear. "I am so proud of you." "Why?" I asked. I put my books away and closed my locker. "Well, because you helped that boy and…" I interrupted her. "Did I really help him? What did I do? I held his hand and watched him die?" She said, "No, you stood by him and tried to help him. You were really brave." I laughed. "What's so funny?" she asked. I laughed again and said, "That wasn't brave. It would have been brave to tell the police what happened and who killed him. No, what I did wasn't brave at all." She touched my arm. "Don't be too hard on yourself. That guy had a gun. There could have been two people shot that day. I'm so glad that nothing happened to you. I don't know what I would have done if he had shot you too." I looked at her and said, "Yeah, you're right. Only one person got shot, only one person will have a funeral, but two people still died that day."

We went to lunch and decided to sit off to the side away from everyone else. "No matter what you say, you were really brave. I am so proud of you," she said. "Thanks…," I replied nonchalantly. She continued. "No…really…I mean it…you were so brave to run out there like that." "Thanks," I replied again. I was getting tired of talking and thinking about it. I just wanted to move on because the more I thought about it, the more agitated I became. I tried changing the subject. "So how long you been going here?" I was looking down at my plate and for a moment, I lost my appetite. I was playing with the cheese on my pizza as she spoke. "I've been here all year..." she adjusted her glasses and then continued, "You probably didn't notice me. It's not like I'm the 'noticeable' type." I looked up and staring into her eyes, I said, "I noticed you." I smiled. She smiled back. We were exchanging smiles when out of the corner of my eye, I saw Niecie walking towards me. I dropped my head because I knew what was going to happen next and it wasn't going to be good. If Niecie was nothing else, she was predictable.

She had two of her 'girls' with her. I closed my eyes and said a silent prayer in hopes that her and her entourage would disappear, but when I opened my eyes, she was still there. Smacking a mouth full of gum, she started right in on me. "Who is this TKO?" She looked in Toni's direction. Toni extended her hand. Niecie didn't take her hand. Instead, she looked at her 'girls' before taking the gum out of her mouth and placing it in Toni's hand. Toni drew her hand back, slowly, looking at the gum in her hand. She looked at me. Then she looked back at the gum in her hands. She took the gum and wiped it on a napkin. Niecie and her friends laughed. "Where did you find this nerd?" one of the girls said. "Yeah, I didn't know that Ugly…ummmm, what is your name?" the other girl said. With tears forming in her eyes, Toni said, "My name is Toni…that's Toni with an 'i'." The girl continued, "It's Ugly Toni…that's Ugly

Toni with an 'i'…okay, Toni?" The girls were laughing when Toni looked at me with eyes that were pleading for me to rescue her. Then I said, "You hags better back the hell up out of my girl's face." Niecie's mouth fell open and her friend's eyes bulged out of their heads. "Your girl," Niecie said. "Your girl?" Toni asked, smiling and wiping the tears from her eyes. "Yeah, my girl," I confirmed. One of the other girls said, "Did he just call us a hag? What the hell is a hag?" The other girl shrugged her shoulders with a confused look on her face. Niecie said, "Sorry about that Bro'…I didn't mean to do that…I'll see you at home." She walked away dragging her friends with her. Toni looked at me. "That was your sister?" I watched them as they walked away. "Yeah…that's my sister."

Chapter 17

Three people were shot while thousands gather to march against the senseless violence in Chicago…

She was sweet; not hard like most of the girls I knew. She was sweet like the sunrise…sweet like the dew that's left on a flower after a storm…she was sweet like a rainbow or like a cold can of pop on a hot summer's day. She was sweet in an innocent kind of way. She was so sweet that I felt that she needed to be protected by someone like me and I wanted to be the one who would shield her from all of the "ugly" in the world.

As I walked her home from school, I imagined what she would look like when she got older – like my mom's age. I could imagine her coming home from work to me. She would throw her arms around me and tell me all about her day and I would listen and hang on to every word.

Everything about her was sincere and genuine – from the hairs on top of her head to the bottom of her feet. She laughed at something she said. I smiled imaging waking up to that smile for the rest of my life. I knew that I was too young to be thinking about marriage with a girl that I barely knew, but something about our meeting each other was destined…ordained, I believed, by God because when she spoke to me her words didn't just touch my ears, but my heart.

When we arrived at her front door, we stopped to look at each other. "That was cool the way you stood up to your sister for me," she said. "Not a problem. She needed to be put in her place...fronting like that....trying to call somebody ugly... I know what she looks like when she wakes up...she has a lot of nerve to try to talk about somebody." I thought about what I said for a minute and embarrassed, I said, "Not trying to say that you're ugly or anything." She tapped me on the hand and said, "I know what you're trying to say, silly." I looked at my hand as I enjoyed the slight stinging feeling. I looked at her. "I needed this...thank you for hanging out with me." She smiled. "That's what

friends are for." "Friends?" I asked. She
smiled and said, "I'm too young for a
boyfriend, but I appreciate you taking
up for me." My dreams of having her as
my future wife were crushed. She saw
the disappointment on my face. She
stood on her tippy-toes, leaned in and
then kissed me on my cheek. I felt the
coolness of the trace of spit left on my
face. I smiled as it dried and soaked into
my skin. She was opening her door,
when she stopped and said, "Let's get to
know each other a little better before we
start talking about boyfriend and
girlfriend." "Sure," I responded. We
were staring at each other when we
heard the sound of a horn coming from
the street. We both looked in its
direction. A red car moved slowly down
the street. We both watched as the car
disappeared down the street. Breaking

the silence, she asked, "Who was that?" I scowled as I watched it until it was out of sight. "No one," I responded. I looked at her to find that she was still watching the car as well. I touched her shoulder to redirect her attention back to me. She smiled. I smiled back. *Just sweet*, I thought to myself, smiling. "Maybe you can stop by and we can walk to school together?" she asked. "Sure," I said, happy that I was being given the opportunity. Her braces caught some of the light from the sun and her smile glistened. "I will be here first thing in the morning."

On my way home, I thought about how a tragedy had turned into something so special. I met Toni and I didn't know how the shooting connected us to this moment in our lives, but I wasn't going to question it any longer. I was just going to enjoy the moment.

As I approached a storefront on one of Chicago's busiest streets, I noticed that the streets were unusually quiet like the world had ended and I was the only person left behind. I thought this was kinda strange, so I began to walk faster. When I approached an alley, out of nowhere, someone grabbed me by the arm and pulled me in. I stumbled and as I tried to catch my footing, I looked around to find that I wasn't alone. There were four other young men in that alley – all staring at me. One of them spoke first. "Well, what do we have here? Look man…," he said as he pointed at one of the others. "It's Mr. Badass from the library…remember?" One of them, said, "Yeah, I remember…" At this point they had me surrounded and the idea of running was out of the question. He continued,"…swooped in like a super hero trying to save ol' boy…acting all tough and shit…yeah, you punched me…hit me pretty hard…I owe you something…don't I?"

I closed my eyes and shook my head in disbelief. *Damn.* I knew these boys. They were from the library. I couldn't believe this shit was happening. One of them spoke. "Now look at you…swing now motherfucker." I looked him up and down. I stopped when out of the corner of my eye, I saw someone walking towards me. "You remember me don't you?" one of them said. I looked at him and as if I traveled back in time, I was standing face-to-face with the killer. Frightened, I began to move toward the entrance of the alley when one of them stopped me cold in my tracks by flashing the handle of a gun at me that stuck out of his pants. *Shit*, I thought to myself. "Where are you going?" he asked. Taking a few steps backwards, I found myself surrounded by them. "I asked you a question…,"the killer said. Surveying the area for a possible way to escape, I replied, "Yeah, I know you." He smiled. "I know you do. We all know each other. We're like one big happy family" he said. *Family?* I thought to myself. *Motherfucker please.*

"Now that we've gotten that out of the way, you're probably wondering why I called you to my office…" Confused, I looked around me. *Called? Office? I* thought to myself. I was afraid, but I wasn't going to show it. *Animals smell fear and when they do, they attack.* Becoming agitated, I said, "Dude, what the hell do you want? I have shit to do." They all looked at each other before breaking out in a laugh so hard that it made me laugh too. Now, we were all in the alley, surrounded by garbage, and laughing like old friends. One of the young men spoke. "Dude? Where the fuck you from? Bellaire? Huh, Carlton?" They laughed for a few seconds longer when suddenly, they all stopped laughing and stared at me - the only person still laughing and looking like a complete idiot. One of the young men said, "You got some shit to do. That's funny." They all laughed again. Getting back to the business at hand, the killer said, "You're probably wondering why I killed ol' boy." Frowning, I lied and said, "No, I wasn't wondering about that at all. Now, like I said, I have things to do." The killer smiled and then walked closer. "Well, I bet you're wondering why I didn't kill you." I stood there looking at him and remembering that day and how close he was to me, holding that gun, daring me to move or say something – anything that would give him a reason to pull the trigger. I thought about it. On that day, he could have erased 16 years of my life…16 years of birthdays…16 years of holidays spent with my family…16 years of sunrises and sunsets. Sixteen years of laughing at my father's stale jokes and pretending that they were funny…11 years of hanging out with my sister…16 years of "I love you" from my mama. In a blink-of-an-eye, it could have all been over. He spoke, interrupting my thoughts. "Yep, there's a reason you ain't dead and I'm going to tell you what that reason is." One of them laughed and said, "The suspense is killin' me, boss." I looked at him, frowned and then said, "I give…why didn't you kill me?" The killer smiled and said, "I am so glad that you asked…I need you to do me a favor." "You need me to do you a favor? You need ME…to do YOU…a favor? What is the favor?" They all stared at me like they were expecting me to read their minds. Becoming extremely annoyed, I continued, "Damn dude, spit that shit out…I don't have all day." He walked up to me and then pulled the gun from his pants. "You have as much time as I give you…you hear me? Now, you know that big church that you go to…well, we want you to rob it."

I choked on air. "What the hell? Dude, I can't rob no church…are you serious?" Smiling, he said, "DUDE, I'm dead serious…don't I look serious?" I looked at him. Yes, he looked very serious. "That fucking preacher riding around in that Mercedes…his wife and her Jaguar…with their fancy clothes, fine home and expensive jewelry…yeah, I want you to take some of that shit." He "fist-bumped" one of them. "They got too much of it anyway. We out here in the streets, struggling, and hustlin' while their asses live like celebrities. Shit, I can't even hate on them. It's the biggest con in the world and we want a piece of the action." They laughed. He continued. "Man, they got it good. That is a sure-fire paycheck…every week. Them preachers have it all figured out – selling pipe-dreams and information that you can get for free. The shit that they are selling creates more zombies than crack and those motherfuckers never see a day in jail for it. They don't have to sell their drug one bag at a time…Naw, those church folks gather together on Sunday morning like they're going to see the Super bowl…it be hundreds and thousands of them…rain or shine…with pockets full of money to give away to a person living better than them. Damn, those church folk are dedicated…and loyal." He shook his head, paused, rubbed his chin, and then said, "I wonder if we could recruit a few of them." Frowning, I said, "They wouldn't join a gang." The killer said, "Why not? It would be like home to most of them and what I do is no different than what a preacher does...they just figured out how to make a ton of money doing it. Shit, I heard that one of them preachers threatened to take the folks that didn't pay-up outside to shoot them. That's no different from what I would have done except, I probably wouldn't have made a video confession of it. That's stupid as hell. Shit, if you ask me, I think that I would make a damn fine preacher." He turned to his friends and said, "Amen?" His friends, shouted, "Amen!" and started waving their hands in the air like they were at church. "Man, stealing from them will be like...it'll be like *Peter Pan*...taking from the rich and then giving to the poor." Shaking my head, I said, "Don't you mean, *Robin Hood*?" One of his friends laughed and then said, "Dude, you just called him a fairy." The killer pointed the gun in his friend's face. "Who the hell you calling a fairy?" His friend threw his hands in the air and then said, "No...no...*Peter Pan*, man...is a fairy...I'm not calling anybody a fairy." "You better not," he scowled and then turned back to me. I shook my head. *Dumbasses*. I thought to myself. "Yeah...you'll be like *Robin Hood*...taking from the rich and giving to the poor." Shaking my head, I asked, "How do you expect me to pull this off?" "Well...you got an ed-u-mo-cation...figure that shit out," he said. "Man, I can't do that...I'll go to jail...," I said. He replied. "Hey...it's the destiny of a Black man...jail or death...why you gon' be different? Huh, college bound? You think you different? Shit, look around you. You steal from or destroy one church, they'll only build another one. Shoot, we have more of them than hospitals and schools and look at our community…a fine place it is. I would want to raise my kid here." He pointed at the buildings around us like he had been appointed the ghetto tour guide. "Which kid?" his friend asked. "You got a lot of them." His friends laughed, but I didn't find any of this shit funny. The killer grabbed my shoulder and then said, "How about this? You do it or we pay a visit to your pretty little sister…what's her name again?" "Niecie," one of the other boys said. Shaking his head and smiling, he said, "Yeah, Niecie…I see her at school sometimes…that chick is mighty fine…kinda uppity…nothing a little back-breaking by me and my boys couldn't fix. Yeah, she'll love that and after we're done, we'll make a bet to see which one of us gets her pregnant. Shit, I got about six kids…" One of the other young men interrupted. "Man, you got eight of them little motherfuckers." The killer looked at him and then smiled. "I stand corrected. I got eight of them little motherfuckers according to the fucking 'Census Bureau' over there…who seems to wanna keep count and shit." They all laughed. He looked at me and smiled. "Now, do as you're told…I don't wanna have to hurt that girl…she looks like she might have some dreams or something and it would be a shame to get them all fucked-up because you want to act like a man." I frowned and said, "Man, you can't touch my sister." He smiled back and said, "Look who's trying to tell me who I can and cannot touch….okay, do you like surprises?" I frowned and said, "What?" "Do you like surprises?" he repeated. I just stood there without responding. I was getting really tired of this shit. When he didn't get a response, he said, "If I don't get what I want then I'll just pay a visit to your home and we'll just pick somebody to pay for your disobedience. Mama, daddy, sister, dog…whoever the hell is at home." When he said the word "disobedience", a chill ran down my spine. Suddenly, I could hear my father's voice saying, *Boy! Didn't I tell you to mind your own business?* Right now, more so than when all of this began, I wish I had.

They were leaving the alley when one of the boys looked over his shoulder and then said, "I told you that we would see each other again." The killer was walking behind them. He stopped, turned, looked at me, and said, "Oh, by the way, they call me Snooky – that's what all the ladies call me."

What gangster calls himself, Snooky? I could see it now…Reverend Snooky. I shook my head. *Punkass.* I thought to myself.

Chapter 18

13 year old Black male, shot and killed in the Woodlawn area…

What am I going to do? How the hell did I get here? How the hell did a visit to church end-up like this? I was in deep shit and didn't know what to do. I couldn't tell anybody because if I did all hell would break loose. If I told my parents they would force me to tell the police and then the police would go looking for him and if they couldn't find him, he would spend the rest of his life trying to get back at me for being a snitch. Even, if I rat on him and he goes to jail, I will be looking over my shoulder for the rest of my life because he had friends and I was sure that there were a lot of them. Damn, this was so messed-up. Why was I chosen – why was I the one who went running to help that young man when all of those people saw the same thing, but there I was…playing hero and now, I will pay the price for it.

That evening at dinner, I was quiet. I had a lot on my mind. Everyone talked about their day as I thought about the mess that I was in. Niecie was laughing when I looked at her, remembering what Snooky said that he would do to her if I didn't rob the church. She caught me staring. With a mouth full of chewed-up food, she stuck her tongue

out at me. *Gross.* I frowned and then
looked back at the food on my plate.
"What's up big brother? You still mad at
me for what happened at school?" she
asked. "What happened at school?" my
mother asked. I didn't want to talk
about it. I just wanted to eat and go to
bed. I didn't respond. My mother asked
again. "What happened at school?"
Frustrated, I said, "Nothing…okay?"
The whole room fell silent. My father
spoke. "I'm not sure what is going on,
but it doesn't give you the right to be
disrespectful." I took a deep breath and
then said, "You're right…it isn't her
fault…I'm sorry mama." She leaned
over and began to rub my back. "It's
okay son…I understand." Looking at
her, I said, "Can I go to bed?" Are you
sure that you don't want to talk about
it?" she asked. I stood and said, "No…I

just want to go to bed." I was walking out of the room when they all shouted, "Good-night!"

The next couple of days went on without a problem. Toni and I spent a lot of time together. We laughed so much that I almost forgot that I had a bunch of criminals expecting me to rob a church. As bad as the situation was, I tried to enjoy life. Deep down, I was still hoping that it would just go away, but that was unlikely. No matter what I did, something bad was going to happen. Things didn't look good for me.

Chapter 19

15 people shot – a mother of two killed…

I prayed every day in hopes that it would all go away, but that didn't happen. One day after getting home from school, I heard someone shout from behind me, "Dude, tell your sister that I said, 'Hi!'" When I turned around, I caught a glimpse of the faces in the car. I recognized the killer's face. I couldn't see the people in the backseat because of the tinted glass, but the driver looked familiar. They took off down the street. I stood there, watching them, until the car was out of sight.

I was both pissed and annoyed after seeing them, but determined not to let them bother me – just for the moment. I knew that I couldn't run from them forever, but for that moment, I just wanted to forget them.

When I walked in the house, I noticed that no one was at home. For the first time, I was alone. It felt good to be alone. I decided to enjoy the peace and quiet. First, I stopped by the kitchen and made a turkey sandwich. I took a bite. I chewed slowly savoring every bite. For I learned, that you must savor everything – never take things for granted, try to enjoy and make all of the good times last for although, tomorrow maybe promised for others, your life can end in an instant – putting an end to all of your tomorrows. As I ate the sandwich, I took a minute to look around the room. It looked strange to me. It's funny how I never really looked at the kitchen before that day. Everything matched – from the towel that hung on the rack to the wallpaper on the walls. The pattern was the same throughout - there was an image of a house, painted in all white, surrounded by a beautiful garden, with flowers of all colors sprinkled all over it. There were butterflies and small little blue birds flying near the garden. It looked so peaceful. Then my thoughts went back to the "streets" where there were no gardens and sprinkled everywhere were liquor stores, churches, and people with nothing better to do, but nothing. Then I thought about Snooky and his demand.

As I sit there with that crap looming over me like a dark cloud, I kinda wish that he had just pulled that trigger. I know that wishing that I died on that day is extreme, but the Bible tells us that "the wages of sin is death." I lied to protect a murderer and that's a sin and I refuse to go out committing another sin. If I was going to go, I won't do it by disrespecting my parents and God by taking money from the church and giving it to a low-life that was probably only going to buy some gym shoes, or some jewelry with it. I didn't care what his plans were, I knew mine didn't include stealing – from anybody.

I closed my eyes and tried to clear my thoughts. That didn't work so I decided to pray for peace because my thoughts were in a bad place. I put my hands together and began to pray, but nothing happened. I drew a blank. I couldn't pray. For the first time in my life, I couldn't remember the Lord's Prayer. I opened my eyes to make sure that I wasn't dreaming or having an out-of-body-experience. I closed my eyes, again, and folded my hands thinking that my actions would jog my memory, but nothing and then I heard a voice say, "When all else fails, speak from your heart." So I took a deep breath and said, "Father, in Heaven, this is Tijani, but I guess that you already know that…" I paused for a moment to collect my thoughts and then continued. "Okay, so you know what's been going on and…the Devil is trying to wreak havoc in my life…He's trying to break me down by threating to attack what I love, but…it can't happen. So many people are dying, Lord…I just ask you Father to watch over us…we can't fight this battle without you. All I know is

Lord, we…I need your help. I need you to step in Lord because…" I paused and then said, with all of the guarantee that a promise could hold, "I will get him before he gets a chance to get us….amen."

After that, I went upstairs to lay my head down for a minute. I was laying there for about an hour when I heard the door downstairs open. The family was making a lot of noise. Now, normally I would have ignored them, but in the distance, I could hear someone crying. I listened closely. It was my mother and she was upset over something. I jumped from my bed and ran downstairs to find my mother standing in the middle of the floor with her clothes shredded about her body. I pushed my father out of the way. I grabbed my mother and held her in my arms. "What happened?" I asked. "It was nothing," she responded, pushing away from me.

"Nothing!" my father shouted. "Nothing! Look at you!" My father paced while I took inventory of the situation. "Okay mama, clearly something happened...what?" She picked up her purse which had the handle ripped from it and said, "Nothing...now, I don't want to talk about this any longer." She began to search her purse for something. Whatever it was, when she found it, she grabbed it tightly in her hand without letting any of us see what it was. She placed it close to her chest and then mumbled something to herself. She left her purse and walked toward the stairs.

Before going up, she said, "I'm alive and I'm okay…there's no need to discuss this any further. Now, I'm going to take a shower and then go to bed."

I waited until she was out of sight before I turned and said, "Dad, what happened?" Frustrated, he replied, "Hell if I know…that stubborn woman won't tell me because she knows that I will walk through fire wearing a pair of gasoline drawers to get to those motherfuckers." I was shocked to hear my father use that word. He cursed sometimes, but words like that were never used, so I knew that he meant what he was saying. He started to pace the floor again. I hesitated to ask the next question, but I was trying to find out what happened. "Was she raped?" My father stopped and looked at me with a look that was frightening. I stepped back because I wasn't sure what he was going to do next. "If another motherfucker had touched your mother do you think I would be standing here talking to you? I would have searched under every rock, searched every sewer, looked into every dirty hole in this city until I found his ass and when I did…oh my God so help me…the things that I would do to him would make the likes of Gacy and Dahmer blush…do you hear me?" That comment was disturbing. The fact that my father just compared what he would do to another man to what Gacy and Dahmer did was frightening because they raped and killed their victims, but I blew it off because I knew where he was coming from. He was angry and had every right to be. I asked, "So what are we going to do?" He looked beaten and tired. "Nothing, but respect your mother's wishes." "So that's it?" I asked. "That's it," he replied and then walked out of the room. I stood there feeling completely helpless. I couldn't understand why she wouldn't tell us what happened. Maybe she thought that we would do something stupid and go after the person who hurt her and maybe we would, but you can't just let someone hurt you and remain quiet about it. *Damn.* As soon as I said it, I was reminded of my situation. For a moment, I felt horrible and confused, but then I understood what she was going through.

I went upstairs to check on my mother. I knocked on the door and there was no answer. "Mama," I said, gently, but there was still no answer. I cracked the door a little before walking in. "I'm coming in mama...I hope that you're decent." There was still no answer. I walked in, carefully as not to walk in on her dressing or startle her. There she was – sprawled out across her bed, sleeping peacefully. I walked over to her bed to place some blankets over her and I looked down to see that she was holding something shiny in her hand. I looked closely to see what it was. Opening her hand slightly, I saw it – it was a cross.

I started crying so hard that it woke her. Jumping up out of her sleep, she said, "Who is that?" Looking in my direction, she said, "Child, what are you doing in here?" I was crying so hard that I couldn't answer her. She walked over and kneeled down beside me.

"Tijani…I'm going to be okay…I'm just a little shaken up…you hear me? I'm okay." She rubbed my shoulders trying to comfort me. I continued to cry. Suddenly, I spoke, but I wasn't making any sense. "Mama…I was stupid…I don't know what to do… everything …just crazy…just crazy…" She began to pat the back of my hand. "Child, take a deep breath and tell me what's going on. I can't understand a word that you're saying." I tried again, this time blurting out the first thing on my mind. "There is no God!" As soon as I said it, I regretted it, but at that moment, it felt true. With all of the things that were happening in my life, His lack of intervention had to mean that He didn't care, He wasn't listening, or He didn't exist.

My mother fell backwards clamping her hand to her chest. "Blasphemy!" She crawled toward me and said, "We have time…come on let's pray…He will forgive your moment of insanity." She tried reaching for my hands and I snatched them from her and with tears in my eyes, I said, "Look at you…even when He turns His back on you…when He doesn't protect you, you still believe…" I looked down at her hand. She looked down too. I continued, "We pray…we worship…we learn and live by His word and what? We are still praying, crying and dying…no matter how much good stuff we do, bad stuff still happens to us. Look at you…you're more faithful than anybody I know and He turned His back on you and allowed the Devil and his soldiers to attack you." I shook my head. "It doesn't make sense." She stood and walked over to the bed and sat down. She took a deep breath and then said, "What else do we have?"

"Huh?" I asked. "What else do we have?" she asked again. Without waiting for an answer, she said, "Tijani…I think that I understand where you are coming from. We all ask the question, 'Why do bad things always happen to good people…to the Lord's people?' I can't answer that. I want to believe that like in the story of Job, we will all be tested at some time in our lives and those who believe in Him will pass the test and will receive His grace and mercy and those who fail? Well…I hear that it gets hot where they are going." She laughed, but then said, "We have to believe in something…in someone…we have to believe and hope that there is something better than 'this' waiting for us and if we believe and stay true to His word…in the end, we will be rewarded. I don't have to see Him to know that He exists…you are a prime example that He does. We believe in so many things…some make sense and some don't, but again, what else do we have? He is the 'hope' that many of us have. Plus, it feels good to know that something greater than anything I could ever hope for is in store for me…all I have to do is live right. Remember, He didn't intervene when Jesus was whipped and nailed to a cross. They crucified and murdered him. We all have to earn our 'stripes' and doing so won't always be pleasant."

I looked at her. What she said made so much sense. She continued. "People wouldn't just do right if there's no incentive...especially when 'sinning' is easy and often times, it feels really good. Folks need something to keep them in check. There's a fine line between what's right and what's wrong. Without God there's nothing...look around you...do you see what man is capable of? Disease, poverty, death, violence, lies and manipulation...shoot, we wouldn't need God like we do if mankind was different...if we were good. Now, I'm not saying that all human beings are bad, but the bad folks are starting to outnumber the good folks and unless, folks see profit in it, they will never stop folks from killing folks...not when people who make and sell guns...people who build those prisons continue to make the kinda money that they are making. Ain't no real money in saving lives...look at the hospitals and funeral homes...business never been so good. So we continue to pray...that's all that we can do son." She stood, walked over to me and then said, "Always do what's right son...always." I looked at her, nodded my head, and then said, "Sure...I will."

Chapter 20

A 75 year old Black male was found stabbed to death in Calumet Heights...

That Sunday morning, I woke up to a renewed sense of faith. My mother's words touched me and I knew what I had to do. We went to service that morning and I praised God harder than I ever had before. When Toni arrived, she came and stood next to me. When my mother saw her, she smiled. My father looked at me and then gave me the thumbs up. Niecie, who was standing on the other side of me looked at Toni and smiled and waved. I felt so proud and so happy. After service, we all stood in the hall where I introduced my family to Toni. Everything was perfect, until…

When we left the church, we were all standing in the parking lot laughing when I saw him walking slowly in my direction. It was Snooky. "Hey, what's up, dude?" he said. I tried ignoring him, but he wouldn't let me. He became louder, forcing his way into the conversation. "Hey man, don't you want to introduce your friend to the family?" When I looked at my father, he was looking Snooky up and down. Toni and Niecie were off into their own world, but when I looked at my mother's face I knew that something was wrong. She was as pale as a ghost. Snooky extended his hand to her and she drew back her hand. She began to walk towards the car when she said,

"Daddy, let's go." He didn't move. She walked back over grabbed my father by the arm and said, "Let's go…right now!" she ordered. I turned to look at Snooky. He laughed and said, "Daddy? That's cute." Huffing, I said, "You have the balls to come to my church…the very church that you want me to steal from?" "Shhhhhh, lower your voice…you don't want folks to hear ya'…now do you?" Remembering the look on my mother's face, I knew that she knew him and from her expression something bad happened between them. It wasn't like her to be rude. Something wasn't right. Making a fist, I said, "What did you do to my mother? I know that you did something." Smiling, he said, "Oh…so she didn't give you my message…" My eyes widened and my nostrils flared. "You put your hands on my mama? Are you crazy?" I asked, angrily. He leaned in and then continued, "I'm not fucking with you…I'm watching you and I expect you to take care of this soon or I'll be paying her another visit." He smiled and then continued. "I've never had one that old. Maybe she can teach me and my boys some new tricks…what do you think?" I was about to knock the shit out of him when I heard my mother yell, "Tijani, get over here!!!" I looked around and was reminded of where I was. Then I smiled and said, "I won't forget…you'll get what's coming to you real soon. I promise you that." Stepping back, he said, "Good…then I'll see you soon." "Sooner than you think motherfucker…sooner than you think," I mumbled to myself.

When we arrived at home, everyone went into a different direction – into their own rooms. After about an hour, Niecie entered my room without knocking. I threw a pillow at her head. She didn't see it coming, so the pillow hit her in the face. "Ouch butt-wipe…" Throwing it back, she said, "What did you do that for?" Blocking the pillow, I said, "You need to learn how to knock before you come in somebody's room." Walking over and plopping on the bed next to me, she said, "What's wrong with you?" Turning, my back to her, I said, "Nothing, now get out." Pulling on my shirt, she said, "Boy, who are you talking to?" I turned and then pushed her on the floor. "Get out! I mean it! I don't have time to play with you." Standing in front of me, breathing heavily, she said, "I don't know what your problem is, but a good butt-kicking will definitely fix it." She began to roll up her sleeves. She pushed me; so hard that I fell backward. Without thinking, I jumped up and grabbed her by the throat. She grabbed at my hands. I looked at her as she struggled. After realizing that I was hurting her, I released my grasp and fell to the floor. "I'm so sorry, Niecie...please forgive me. I don't know what I was thinking." Pushing away from me, she said, "What the hell is wrong with you? You tried to kill me?" Covering my face with my hands, I said, "I wasn't trying to kill you." Rubbing her neck, she said, "Then what the hell was that?" Pleading, I said, "Please forgive me." "No TKO, you need to explain yourself. You tried to strangle me…what is going on with you?" I paused and then took a deep breath. "Man, I really messed up and because of my mistake, mama got hurt." Niecie stopped rubbing her neck and then looked at me. Her eyes began to twitch. "What do you mean got hurt and by who?" "Remember the guy that I was talking to at the church? Well… he was the person who shot that kid at the church." Niecie looked at me. She began to breathe hard and before I could say anything, she said, "Put your shoes on." I knew what she wanted to do. I looked at her in agreement, but then paused and thought about what would happen if we went after him. She was pounding her fist in her hands and pacing the floor. "Okay…here's what we're going to do. We are going to roll up on him tonight...catch him off guard and..." I interrupted her and said, "Roll up on him with what? Our bare hands? He has guns, Niecie, and he's surrounded by a bunch of his boys who have guns too. After they finish laughing at us, they are going to shoot us both for being stupid." She stopped pacing and then looked at me. "Well, we can't just sit here and let him get away with violating our mama. They put their hands on her and now, we need to put our hands on them." "And then what, Niecie? I agree that something should be done, but what? We roll up on them...they roll up on us...when does it end? Man, you don't know how bad I wish none of this happened...now, it's out of control." I hesitated, but couldn't hold it any longer. "He told me to rob the church."

Walking over to me, she said, "What? He wants you to do what?" "He wants me to rob the church," I repeated. Then I said, "If I don't, he's going to hurt you guys…one by one." Niecie sat down next to me. "Damn, this is messed up." "I know, right?" I sighed. "I don't know what to do." Then she said, "And if you tell somebody, we may all still get hurt or even killed. Man, this is so freaking messed-up." "I know," I confirmed. Looking at me, she said, "We just need to figure out how to get out of this." I stood and walked toward the door. "Look, I got us into this and now, I'm going to get us out." She looked at me and then said, "Why is he messing with you? I don't get it. All of the people in the world and he ask you to rob a church. Why?" I sighed. "Because…he let me live," I said.

Chapter 21

62 years old Black female found shot to death in Burnside...

I couldn't sleep. I tossed and turned all night. My thoughts were racing and the more I thought about everything that happened the more restless and angry I became.

That motherfucker put his hands on my mama. As a man, you don't let that type of shit slide. AND he admitted the shit to my face. What does he take me for? Some punkass who will just cower and look pass that type of shit...? You lied. You lied. Remember you lied. *He thinks that I am scared of his ass because I didn't report him to the police, but he put his hands on my mama…he made a threat against my mama…motherfuckers get killed over that shit. That's an unforgiveable offense. His ass is going to be dealt with before they roll out the evening paper. No motherfucker is going to roll-up on my mama, hurt her and then disrespect her…that's a no-no.*

Now, how was I going to handle this? I jumped out of bed and began to pace the floor looking for an answer and then it came to me. *He thinks that he's tough 'cause he's got a gun…well, he won't be the only motherfucker with a gun. His ass wouldn't be nothing without that gun. I would sweep the streets with his ass.* "Eye for and eye…that's how he wants to handle this? Since he touched my mama then maybe, somebody need to pay his mama a visit?

Before I could talk myself out of it, I was out of the door and determined as hell. No one could stop me from finding what I needed. I was going to finally put an end to all of this mess. As I walked the streets looking for someone who might be selling a gun thoughts ran through my mind, but I ignored them. The good inside of me kept trying to talk me out of it, but I was pissed. I knew that a part of being a man was being able to protect my family. I wasn't going to let that punk destroy my family. Then something inside of me said, "A man knows how to defend his family without having to pull a trigger and if you kill that young man then you will be the one destroying your family and not him."

I stopped and then fell to my knees. I covered my face with my hands. *What am I going to do?* I thought to myself. I felt so alone. I felt like giving up. I didn't know who I could turn to. Strange, but in that moment, Brenda came to mind. I don't know why, but the more I thought about it – the more that I thought about her.

When I returned home, I searched the house for the address of the prison that she was being held at. After looking in one of Niecie's drawers, I found a letter that had the return address on it. I walked into my room and closed the door behind me. After gathering a few sheets of paper, I sat down to write Brenda a letter.

I looked at those pieces of paper for what seemed like a lifetime. Then I placed the pen to the paper and began to write the first thing that came to my mind. *We need you...I need you.* I didn't waste any time on the normal things that had happened in my life. Instead, I kept it simple – told her what was happening and then asked her for her help. When I was done, I folded the letter, placed it into the envelope, addressed it, and then hurried to place it into the mailbox.

After I placed it in the mailbox, I stood there – staring at it like I was expecting some kind of confirmation that I did the right thing, but nothing happened. All I could do from that moment on was hope and pray that something good would happen.

It was almost a week later before I received a response in the mail from Brenda.

I opened the letter. It read:

Go to the police. Tell them what happened. Let them take care of this. Remember what I told you when you were little? You don't want to be like me when you grow-up kid. Do what's right. Always, do what's right. Tell my baby that I love her.

Go to the police? Be a snitch? That was totally against everything that I'd learned. Why would she tell me to go to the police when she knew what would happen if I did, but I had to trust her because she knew that my actions could hurt all of us; even Niecie and if she was telling me to go to the police then she knew what she was doing.

Without thinking about it for another second, I got dressed and ran out of my house. Determined, to put an end to this madness I just had to let go and trust God. I ran until I found myself standing in front of the police station. When I walked in I knew that I was in the right place because a person walked up to me and said, "You look like you could use some help...how may I help you?" A weight was instantly lifted from my shoulders. I pulled the officer off to the side and told her briefly what was troubling me. She took me to a room and introduced me to a detective who listened to me and showed me some pictures. When I was done he said, "We've been trying to catch that guy for a while, but every time we get close...we never have enough evidence to hold him and no one is willing to speak up. I'm glad that you came in." "Me too," I replied. "Do you need a ride home?" he asked. "Naw, I better not get caught getting out of a cop's car, but thanks anyway." He stood to shake my hand. "Don't worry...we're going to take care of this...thanks for coming in." "No problem," I said before I left.

On my way back home, I could only think about what I had just done. I was afraid before I walked in the police station, but now, my fear had heightened to a whole new level. You never snitch. That is the code of the streets, but if I didn't the repercussions for remaining silent were far more greater. If I didn't speak up, I would live in fear for the rest of my life, but the result could be the same for speaking up. At least this way, if something happened to me the police would know who to look for.

That night, I couldn't sleep. I tossed and turned until I found myself staring into the darkness. As I laid there, I thought about Brenda's advice and wondered if going to the police was the right thing to do. The more I thought about her advice and the situation, the tired and frustrated I became of it all. I felt so powerless. I couldn't understand how a good deed could turn into this. As I struggled with trying to make sense of everything, I heard a loud popping sound come from outside. I thought that it was firecrackers, so I ignored it. Suddenly, the sound became louder as it got closer to the house. I rolled out of bed and unto the floor. Carefully, I looked out of my window to find a red car parked in front of my house. One of the passengers, held his hand out of the car's window. He was holding something –waving it back and forth. The light from the moon bounced off the object. It was silver. It was a gun. He pulled the trigger several times causing a popping sound. I ducked behind the window sill. He shot the gun five times into the air before they sped off into the night.

Chapter 22

A 7 year old Black female was shot and
killed in the Austin area...

The church planned a trip to the amusement park. I didn't want to go. I was tired; physically and mentally. The only thing that I could think about was the night before and all of the dumbshit that I've gotten me and my family into. I wasn't in the mood to have fun or anything else for that matter. I didn't want to be here. I didn't want to be any place where my family and I couldn't be protected. But even if I told them what was going on, we couldn't run from the evitable. Nothing can protect you from people who have no value or respect for life. In their world, the rules are different. You did what they told you to do or you had to pay the price and the price for disobedience was pain or death. Then you had to believe them and nothing could protect you from the punishment. Killing, stealing, and destroying was all in a day's work for them.

Toni's family hung out with my family the entire day. I was glad that they had. It was a welcomed distraction. I needed something – I needed her to help take my mind off of things; even if it was just for a day. As we ran from ride to ride, everyone laughed. They were having such a good time; unaware of the danger that they face because of me. Every time someone screamed, I jumped. Every time there was a loud sound, I jumped. This was no way to live.

At lunch, Toni and I drifted away from our families to be alone. We were talking and laughing – sharing story after story about our childhood. She told me a story that had something to do with something called, Binky.

She began. "When I was little, I used to love my pacifier. I took it everywhere. Well, when I got too old for it my mom tried to wean me off of it, but I only turned to sucking my fingers. She hated it. She tried everything. She covered my hands with socks. She dipped my fingers in hot sauce…everything. Until one day she got tired of looking at me with my fingers stuck in my mouth. She took my hand and then soaked it in something called Mineral Oil." She

paused to laugh. "Man, you talking
about gross and it gave me the runs
something terrible." I watched as she
buckled over in laughter. "Boy, I was
sick as a dog all night long."

The story wasn't funny, but watching
her laugh made me want to laugh too,
but I couldn't. There she was, laughing
because she got diarrhea and all I could
think about was dying. When I didn't
laugh at her story, she asked. "What's
wrong?" I didn't answer her. We
walked a little further until we
approached an old tree sitting in the
middle of the park. When we got closer
to it, she said, "You want to carve our
names in the tree?" I frowned and said,
"How many people do you know do
that?" "Two," she replied. "Because me
and you are carving our names in this

tree AND we are going to draw a heart around it AND you are going to like it." There was something cute in her trying to boss me around and even though I didn't want to do it, I did.

I looked around to make sure that no one I knew could see me standing there carving a heart in a tree. Looking on the ground, I found a rock and began to carve our names in the tree and then I drew a heart around them. I stood back to look at my handy work. It looked good. I smiled. I was about to throw the rock on the ground when Toni grabbed me by the collar, pulled me to her level and kissed me. When our lips first made contact, I was so in shock that I didn't close my eyes immediately. It was after a few seconds when what was happening began to sink in. My first kiss and it was with the girl I loved. *I loved?* Yes, I loved this girl and as we shared our first kiss I knew that being alive to share more kisses would be the only thing that mattered from this point on.

We sat under the tree and talked about our plans for the future. She was rambling off a list of colleges when I interrupted her. "Toni, I have something I want to tell you." She stopped talking and then turned to look at me. "Why so serious, Tijani? What's going on?" I sighed and took her hands into mine. "Remember when that boy got shot at that church?" I asked. "Sure," she said.

"Remember that guy who walked up to me holding that gun?" She looked away and said, "I really didn't get a chance to see his face." I looked at her in disbelief. "So you didn't see him?" I asked. Looking at the ground, she said, "No, not really. My dad pushed me and my mom back into the church...and ummmm..." I was disappointed to hear that. I couldn't believe that she was doing this – pretending not to have seen him, but I couldn't judge her and I couldn't prove what she may or may not have seen. "It's cool. You don't have to admit that you saw him." She looked up and said, "No, I really didn't see him." I looked deep into her eyes. Something in them told me that she was telling the truth, so I let it go. "Well, he could have killed me, but decided to keep me alive because..." I hesitated and then said, "… because he wants me to rob the church." With a surprised look on her face, she said, "He wants you to do what? Have you told your parents?" I replied, "No, Toni, listen to me…I'm not going to do it, but he threatened to hurt my family and…he's already hurt my mother…""He what?!!!"she asked. "Yes, but…let me finish. I was going to buy a gun…" "You were going to do what?!!!"she said, excitedly. Trying to calm her down, I said, "Look, I didn't…I told the police what happened instead." Calming down a little, she said, "You have to tell your parents." Shaking my head, I said, "I can't. It would really make them mad. My dad would kill me after finding out that something I did or didn't do got my mama hurt and maybe now that the police know what's happening they will catch his butt and throw him in jail." She folded her arms, and twisted her mouth and said, "Are you serious?" She dropped her arms and started shaking her head in disbelief. "I'm glad that you told the police, but that boy is one murderer in a city full of murderers. They catch him and then what? Your problem might go away for a minute, but his absence will only create a new problem. They will just graduate the next guy in line and the cycle starts all over again and have you thought about what would happen if they don't catch him?" I shook my head "yes." "I've already thought about that, " I said. "AND they find out that you may have snitched?" She asked. "Dropping my head, I said, "Yeah, I've thought about that too." "This is so bad…you know that, right?" she asked.

"Yep, I know it." "Well, we have to tell your parents," she said, standing and taking my hand to pull me up. "Okay, but if they kill me, tell Niecie that I want to wear that blue suit that I took the school pictures in," I joked, trying to lighten the mood. She sighed. "That isn't funny and you know it." My comment upset her and she was right. None of this shit was funny. I apologized, but the look on her face didn't change. She was upset about what I'd told her and I wished that I could say more to comfort her, but nothing I said would be sincere. This shit was bad and I knew it. Now, I was regretting my decision to tell her.

She held my hand as we walked over to where both families were sitting and talking. When we got there, I didn't have to say anything because Toni did all of the talking. Interesting enough, no one interrupted her while she spoke. They just sat there, quietly, until she was done. When she finished, they all looked at me. Toni's father said, "Let's hold hands in prayer and then turn this over and put into God's hands." Every one said "Amen" at the exact same time and then we all held each other's hands. Her father led the prayer. I closed my eyes. During the prayer, Toni held my hand; squeezing it gently. I looked down at her. She looked up – forcing a smile on her face. I smiled back, but she looked away. When he was finished, he said. "It's in God's hands now. It's going to be okay." I looked at him and said, "I hope so."

Chapter 23

23 years old White male, shot and killed near the West-side…

A couple of days later, me, Toni, and Niecie were walking home from school. We were two houses away from our home when I heard the buzzing sound of a lawnmower. I looked up to find my father in the front yard cutting the grass. We waved at him. He smiled and waved back. We were talking and laughing, discussing all of the things that happened that day when a red car pulled up beside us. We were so occupied with each other that we didn't see the three young men jump out of the car. When they did, it startled the girls so bad that they dropped their books. We all kneeled to pick them up. I looked-up at the young men. *Damn, this shit can't be happening.* I dropped my head in disbelief.

Snooky was the last person out of the car. When he jumped out, he had his gun in his hand. I didn't say anything. Niecie and Toni held each other tightly. My head was spinning. I wanted to faint, but my body was so stiff that it wouldn't fall to the ground. Walking up to me, he said, "Boy, so you thought that I was playing with you?" Immediately, I looked to see where Toni and Niecie were. I pulled them until they were standing behind me. Then Snooky continued, "Boy, I'm going to ask you one more time...do you think that I'm fucking playing with you?

Where's my money?" Nervously, I looked around to see if I could get help, but there was no one on the street, but us. I would have signaled for my father to help us, but he had walked to the back of the house and was cutting the grass in the backyard – he couldn't hear us over the sound of the mower. After realizing that I was on my own, I swallowed hard and then said, "No, I didn't think that you were playing with me." Angrily, he pushed my shoulder. "Then where the hell is my money? I know that I was clear with my instructions…you said that you understood and yet, I don't have my damn money." Two of the other young men walked closer. Keeping my eyes on them, I said, "I'm sorry, but I just couldn't do it." Frowning, he said, "So you didn't see what I did to your moms…now, you wanna make me hurt her for real." When he said that, I became angry; still afraid, but angry. I had to think, use my head because I wasn't alone. I could hear Toni crying from behind me as Niecie tried to console her.

This wasn't their fight. I had to keep a cool head so that he wouldn't do something stupid and hurt one of them. I took a deep breath and then said, "Look man…" Before I could finish my sentence, one of the other boys reached behind me and pulled Niecie out by her hair. Toni tried grabbing her, but then one of the boys snatched her by the arm. When I turned to try to stop them, Snooky hit me in the side of my face with the handle of his gun. Collapsing to my knees, I grabbed my face. The side of my face felt like it was on fire. The girls tried to help me, but the other two boys held them back. As I lay on the ground, Snooky and his friends laughed at me. As I rubbed the side of my face, I thought about dying. At that moment, as the realization of what was happening sunk in, the thought of dying didn't frighten me. I knew that my death would finally put an end to all of this. I had accepted my fate and was at peace. If this is God's Will then I had to accept it. I bowed my head and began to pray, silently.

Suddenly, I didn't hear the sound of the lawnmower anymore. I heard a voice cry out. "TKO, what the hell is going on?" I looked up at my father who was walking towards us. "Daddy, no!" I shouted. Then Snooky walked over to where one of them was holding Niecie and he took his hand and slid it between her legs. She screamed and then kicked him in the leg. He fell backwards, but when he recovered he hit her in the face. At this point, my father had picked up a broom and was running towards us. I stuck out my hand to stop him, but it was too late. Snooky turned and looked at my father. My father looked at me. I met his gaze before I heard something pop. We all turned toward the popping sound.

"No!!!!" I cried out. "No!!!" We screamed. My father grabbed his chest and then looked at me. With a confused look on his face, his body fell to the ground. He looked down again at the gunshot wound and then looked at me before closing his eyes. His limp arms fell to the ground.

At first, nothing registered. I didn't move. I grabbed my head and then screamed. At first there was no sound. I couldn't breathe. My mouth was open as I watched in disbelief. Then suddenly as if someone had kicked me in my chest - air and sound escaped my body. "No!!!!" I screamed. With tears in my eyes, I stood and pushed Snooky to the ground. "You shot my father you son of a bitch! You shot my father!" We started to fight. We struggled and the gun went off again. The bullet went into the air. We continued to struggle and then the gun went off again, this time hitting a car door. We continued to struggle when the gun went off hitting a glass window. I balled-up my hand, reached back, and when it came around, it landed right in Snooky's face. We continued to wrestle when I did it again – balled my hand into a fist, reached back, and when it came around, it landed on his face, but it didn't stop him. He still continued to fight me. Turning the gun on me, he pulled the trigger, but nothing happened. When I pushed his hand away, the gun went off again. We looked at each other - both of us were surprised at what happened. I should have been killed, but I wasn't. My life was spared.

Suddenly, I heard someone scream, "Get away from him!!!" I looked up and Toni was running towards us. Snooky turned in Toni's direction. Before we both knew it, Toni had jumped on top of Snooky. The gun flew out of Snooky's hand. They struggled. I stood and jumped in between them – pushing Toni out of the way. Toni landed near the gun. Snooky and I were fighting when Toni said, "Get off of him!" We both stopped and found ourselves starring down the barrel of a gun. We both put our hands up. Toni pointed the gun at Snooky. "Toni, please put the gun down, "I pleaded. She had a crazed look in her eyes. I begged her, "Toni…look at me…please put the gun down." She didn't respond. Snooky, who was sitting next to me said, "Bitch, what you gone do?" She walked closer and said, "What did you call me?" Not moving, he said, "You heard me bitch." Still sitting next to him, I held out my hand. "Toni…don't do it…please, put it down." Toni turned and looked at me. Suddenly, Snooky reached up and tried to take the gun from Toni. Just as he touched her arm, the gun went off. POP! I felt something warm hit my face. Toni fell backwards onto the ground. I closed my eyes and when I opened them, I saw Snooky lying on the ground next to me.

Moments later, we heard sirens. Within seconds, police were everywhere. I stood and ran over to where my father laid motionlessly on the concrete. "Daddy, speak to me...daddy, please speak to me!" Niecie and Toni joined me at his side. Niecie screamed, "Daddy...no please...not my daddy." I took him into my arms and held him close; rocking him back and forth. "Daddy, please don't leave me! Daddy, please don't leave me!" He didn't respond. I looked up and through tears I could see Snooky's body. I looked in his direction, dropped my head, and began to cry.

An officer jumped out of one of the cars before it stopped rolling. "Drop the guns and put your hands in the air!" the officer shouted. Everyone did as they were told.

The paramedics arrived. They rushed over to help my father. They tried pulling him from my arms, but I wouldn't let go. "Son, you have to let us help him." I looked blankly at their faces, looked down at my father, whispered "I'm so sorry, daddy…I'm so sorry," and then released him. At first, it felt like I was trapped in a bad dream, but then I looked down to find my father's blood soaked into my shirt.

I looked around at all of the chaos that was going on. I watched the paramedics as they tried to revive him, but it was too late. He was gone. I saw the police talking to Niecie and Toni. People were screaming. A woman ran out of her house, screaming, "My baby! Somebody help my baby!"

I sat emotionless as the paramedics and the police spoke to me. I was shaken, so shaken that when the officer first approached me, I just stared at him. "Son, are you okay?" I looked at him blankly as voices cried-out all around us. Again, I looked down at my shirt. The officer repeated the question. "Son, are you okay?" With tears in my eyes, I looked up at the officer. "No, I'm not okay…" We both looked around at the crime scene. "Does this shit look okay?"

"The End."

Epilogue

Since January 2012 to July 2012, over 308 people were shot in Chicago. As I look at these numbers, I take a moment to think about why it may be happening and why it is so difficult to stop. The reasons for the violence are many: poverty, lack of mentors and role models, drug activity, increased availability of firearms, an unjust justice system, glamorized racial inequality, gang presence and activity, lack of parental structure and guidance, no respect for authority figures, poor or failing schools systems, and a lack of morals.

Only when it came to freedom did the oppressed rise up against their oppressor but when you hate what is being done to you over-and over again,

with hundreds of years of brain-
washing, the enemy will convince you
that you deserve it and that you have
your own people to blame. Now the
enemy no longer exists externally, but
internally and now that you have been
taught to hate yourself, the enemy now
becomes everyone who looks just like
you; so now the oppressed becomes the
oppressor - the abused will now become
the abuser. You kill, destroy, and
terrorize your own communities and for
each life taken – one must be avenged
and thus the cycle continues.

Wars are started to gain freedoms that
once did not exist. The wars that have
erupted in the streets of Chicago, is just
about bloodshed. If the taking of life
was due to hunger or survival, people
could understand it…not justify it, but

understand it. But no one gains anything when life is taken for no reason. Many claim that it is for respect, but when the blood flows from the chest of a newborn baby – where is the respect in that?

As the walls to the prisons are constantly being filled with the bodies of minorities, as the holes in the cemetery are being dug for those gunned-down in the streets, to the hospitals that patch-up what is left of the broken bodies, to the churches who try to heal the fractured souls – We all suffer. For every life taken, was a life that could have done great things, but now, we will never know. As the word "future" becomes something as abstract and as confusing as the reasons for why all of this is happening, we all look away in fear and confusion until somebody else's baby becomes our own baby.

Other
Available
Books

It's time to keep it real. *Kiss My A@@! – This is Not Your Typical Self-Help Book* is an emotional plea to stop the madness. Until now, we have all sat and watched as things around us came apart at the seams. It is time for us to take a moment, step back, access the chaos, and tell the world exactly how we feel about the crap that is happening in our lives. "This book is about the truth as I see it. I'm not going to sell or tell you something that you already know. I am a firm believer in the truth and I believe that as intelligent individuals we deserve it." This book is not your typical self-help book. It does not hold any profound secrets or intellectual theories.

There are no gray areas or small print. It's a book about life…real life…unscripted. "I am no guru, doctor, counselor, preacher, spiritual adviser, talk show host, or motivational speaker. I am a regular person with regular problems, and an un-regular approach to seeing and dealing with all of it. Life can be unpredictable and at times, I have to remind myself who is in control, so I've decided to fight the battles that I know I can win, turn the difficult ones over to God and everything in the middle can just KISS MY A@@!"

Never What it Seems II – A Mother's Love is a story of sacrifice, dedication, and unconditional love. Dee and AJ, best friends, thrown together by circumstances beyond their control are up against their biggest challenge ever – motherhood. Dee, mother of two adopted daughters, grew-up in a household void of love. She struggles each day to juggle a career and a family that desperately requires twenty-four hour attention, but she can't assume a role foreign to her. Raised in a household with an alcoholic father and an absentee mother, Dee has no idea how to handle these girls who were placed into her life by God to eliminate the loneliness created by a husband, her first love, who betrayed her by living a life on the "down-low." AJ, her best friend and mother of one, is married to the man of her dreams. A union that birthed a beautiful little boy struggles to survive. Born to a father who thought she was put on earth to be his surrogate wife and a mother who sat quietly by, ignoring the screams and cries for help that came from her bedroom at night, AJ wants to love her son, but can't because she doesn't know how. She reaches out to her husband for help, but he's MIA due to situations beyond his control. In a role unfamiliar to them, life and experience will take them on a journey that will lead them back to the place where it all started. Their journey continues...

Fallen Angel is the story of a man. He's someone who walks among us very day. On the outside, he's the picture of perfection, but on the inside there's a war going on. His name is Izrael, biblically, the Angel of Death. He just wants to be left alone as he struggles to deal with the demons of his past – his fears, his guilt, and his regrets. Everyone wants him – to be a part of his world whether willingly or by force. He fights daily to destroy the frightening thoughts that wreak havoc on his ability to find balance and peace of mind. He realizes that in order to survive – a part of him must die. His survival – his redemption depends on it. Join me as we take a

journey with Izrael as he delivers his
message with contempt and conviction.

Autumn Leaves is the story of forbidden love, lies, and deceit. It is a story of self-discovery that engages the readers own definition of love gained and love lost. Claire is in love with the man of her dreams who she plans to marry until a woman walks into their lives and forces her to question herself, her beliefs, and her love for the only person who has always been there for her. Mimi is Claire's best friend. Open about every aspect of her life, Mimi holds a secret that if exposed could change both of their lives forever. In a story of self-reflection, we find a connection in each woman's struggle for definition and truth.

Never What it Seems is the story of Dee Wellington and AJ Madison, two women who were born in Chicago, and much like the city; their lives are anything, but ordinary.

Dee grew up in a dysfunctional household that by today's standards would be considered completely 'normal'. Trying to cope with life's complexities, Dee contributes all of life's changes to God's will. Throughout the changes in her life, she resists the urge to disrupt the balance of things unless she really has to. On the other hand, there is AJ Madison who is a rambunctious, intelligent, and outgoing character who lives by her own standards and believes that you get what you give. Both, Dee and AJ grew-up trying to maneuver in systems created to breakdown the human spirit. Readers will find a familiarity in their struggles, their desires, and their will to overcome.